Thedric's life is neat and tidy. He has his job, his parents, and his wife, and it's been that way for the past twenty years. So what if he yearns for more? So what if he wants love and a real family that will love him the way he imagines families love each other?

Les has watched his nephews meet their mates, and between them and his brother, he's starting to wonder if his time will ever come. He's not lonely, but he does feel alone sometimes, and at forty-four, it feels like he missed his opportunity.

When Thedric allows his brother to drag him to a family birthday party, he doesn't expect to meet his mate, and he doesn't know what to do with Les. Their lives are so different that they feel they can't mesh together, and while Thedric is ready to do everything to make it work, Les is more hesitant.

Can Thedric leave his lavish life behind, or will he bow to his parents' demands that he stay married? And if he does leave his old life behind, can he and Les make it work, or are they too different and set in their ways to welcome a mate in their lives?

Thedric

ISBN: 978-1-4874-3862-3
Cover art by Angela Waters

Published by eXtasy Books Inc

Look for us online at:
www.eXtasybooks.com

Thedric
Green Hill Pride 8

By

Catherine Lievens

Chapter One

Like every time when he was with his parents, Thedric wished he could be anywhere but here. He didn't want to be having dinner with them. Even worse, he had to listen to them rant about their grandson and how everything they'd been planning for Miko had been ruined.

Good.

Thedric nodded at something his mother said, then stuffed a piece of meat into his mouth. At least the cook was just as good as she'd been for the past few years. The food was delicious, and Thedric wondered if the cook would allow him to steal her away from his parents. They weren't enjoying the food, so what did it matter? Thedric would make better use of the cook than they ever had.

"Isn't there anything you can do?" Thedric's mother asked.

He should have listened better so he'd know what she was talking about.

He plastered a neutral expression on his face. "I don't see how there's anything I could do." It wasn't a lie if she'd still been talking about Miko. There wasn't anything Thedric wanted or would do to get the boy under the same bad influence his parents had on him and his brother. Miko was free, and he needed to stay that way.

Thedric would make sure he did.

His mother wrinkled her nose. "But there has to be something. He's our grandson. We had plans for him, and everything is ruined. We need to find another way to get him."

Thankfully, Thedric's parents had only found a way to

contact Miko after he turned eighteen. Thedric wouldn't put it past them to try to get custody of him if he'd been a minor, but there was nothing they could do as it was. Even if Miko were to be declared incompetent, as they'd already tried to do, his parents and his mate would be the ones to take care of him, not his grandparents.

Thedric was thankful for small miracles every day.

He put down his fork and stared at his mother. He didn't want to fight with her because she was passive-aggressive, but he also couldn't let this go. He might not have been in Miko's life for the first nineteen years of it, but that didn't make the boy any less his nephew, and after growing up with his parents, Thedric knew better than most what would have happened if they'd found a way to get their hands on Miko. He was living proof of it.

"We've already gone over this," he said, ignoring the way his mother glared at him. "And even though some of Father's friends tried helping, they didn't get the results you wanted. What makes you think that trying something else will change anything? Miko is an adult, and no matter how hard you try, you won't be able to convince him to obey you. And even if something were to happen to him, he has a mate who'll take care of him."

Thedric's father slammed his wine glass onto the table. The red liquid sloshed but stayed in. Thedric glared at him, but while his mother was passive-aggressive when they bickered, his father was outright aggressive, and that wasn't something he wanted to deal with any more than his mother's behavior.

"That *mate*, as you call him, is human."

"And? It doesn't change what they are to each other, and if I were you, I'd keep my distance. You know how bad the consequences will be if you try to interfere in their mating." Surely, Thedric's father wouldn't be that stupid, no matter what he thought of mates.

Although Thedric wouldn't put it past him to attempt something. His father needed control as much as he needed to breathe. When he didn't control his family, he lost it, which was what had happened with Miko, and before that, when Damick had left.

Thedric remembered well how life had been after his brother had met his mate. Their parents hadn't wanted him to bond with her. She was a Nix, but she wasn't someone they would have chosen for him because she wouldn't benefit them and their status, and they'd made sure he knew that. They'd already had a marriage arranged for him. Everything had been planned down to the number of children he'd been supposed to give them. They'd expected him to let go of his mate and obey their orders, but he hadn't.

Instead, he'd bonded with his mate and moved away without hesitation. He'd never come back.

Thedric and Damick's parents had lost one of their chess pieces, and they hadn't been able to get another one. They'd hoped that with Miko in the picture, that would change, and Thedric was pretty sure his father had already started putting out feelers to find someone to arrange a wedding with, but thankfully, Miko had told Thedric's father where he could put that arranged marriage.

Thedric would have paid for a video of his father's reaction to that.

Both Miko and his father were much stronger than Thedric ever had been. Thedric had gone along with everything his parents had wanted since he was a child, including marrying the person they'd chosen for him. That didn't mean they were happy with him. He could feel his mother staring at him, and he was doing his best to keep his focus on his plate and the food on it.

"Well, if we're not going to get Miko, then we need another child," she said.

Dammit. Thedric had hoped she wouldn't bring this up. "You don't need a child," he said, hoping she'd get the hint.

She might have gotten it, but she ignored it. "It's been twenty years. There is *no* excuse for you and Leiana not to have children yet." She put down her napkin and leaned forward. "It's her, isn't it? For some reason, she doesn't want children." She sucked in a breath. "Or maybe she's unable to have children." She made it sound like it would be the end of the world if that was the case.

Thedric might not be in love with his wife, but that didn't mean he didn't love her in his own way. He would never dare raise his voice at his mother, but neither of his parents could stop him from glaring at her, and he did just that.

"Leave her out of this," he said through gritted teeth. "The decision to have or not have children was one we agreed on. Besides, we have time."

"But we've already missed several arranged marriages. We could have concluded them if you'd had children or even with Miko, but we don't have anything now. We need children."

"And if your wife is a problem, just don't listen to her," Thedric's father said. His smile was smarmy and revolting. "Just do what it takes to get her pregnant. She's your wife. It's her duty to give you children, and what she thinks doesn't matter."

The food Thedric had just eaten threatened to make a reappearance, but he swallowed and hoped that wouldn't happen. He knew what his father was suggesting, and the thought of doing that to anyone horrified Thedric.

Thedric resisted the urge to snap at his father or tell him to fuck off. He never did that, instead always trying to keep the peace. It was the only way for him to have a relationship with his parents, but more and more, he wondered if it was worth it.

What had a relationship with his parents given him? As far as he could see, only negative emotions. Because of them, he'd lost touch with his only brother. He'd missed watching his nephew grow up. He hadn't had a chance to find love because he'd married a woman who'd been chosen for him, and he could only imagine what would have happened if he'd met his mate like his brother had.

Thedric had always been the perfect son. He'd followed his parents' orders because he'd never had the guts to stand up to them. He'd thought it was his duty and that he'd be fine, that this was how things were supposed to be.

Had it been worth it?

Thedric had kept the peace, and the only thing he'd gained from that was loneliness and the feeling that he'd wasted his life. He was successful at his job and enjoyed what he did, or at least he used to. Lately, it felt like the creative side had gone out the window, and he could only focus on the money side of the apps he'd created. That was what his father wanted, and what he wanted was law.

But was it what *Thedric* wanted?

Thedric had some thinking to do. His parents were the only family he had left. He hadn't talked to his brother in a long time, except when his parents tried pulling Miko into their lives. Considering what they'd done, Thedric wouldn't be surprised if Damick refused to see him again. That meant he'd be completely alone if he opposed his parents.

That was what he'd been afraid of since the beginning, but right now, he was starting to feel like that might be preferable to having dinner with his parents on a weekly basis and allowing them to make him miserable.

When Les stepped out of the shower, he felt much better than he had when he'd stepped in. The hot water had helped, but at his age, it was getting harder to feel good by the end of a working day. His job had always been physical, and he was starting to feel the weight of it in his bones and muscles.

But tonight, he didn't have time to commiserate. He had a dinner date, and while it wasn't with anyone he might end up in bed with, that didn't make him any less excited. He loved spending time with his family, and seeing his nephews happy with their mates was worth going to bed a little later than usual. Besides, he worked with one of his nephews. If he had trouble getting up tomorrow morning, he just had to call Niall and tell him he'd be coming in later.

Of course, it would be better if he called Val. As much as Les loved Niall, he had eyes, and he'd been working with his nephew for years. Niall was a great construction worker and an even greater nephew, but he sucked at the administrative part of the job. He was good with his hands and enjoyed working, but when it came to the accounts and the clients, he was useless. That was where his best friend and one of Les's favorite people in the world came in.

Val would be perfect to step into Les's shoes eventually. Les had every intention of leaving the business to him once he decided he was too old to continue working, and he'd been training him for that. He hadn't told him about it, and he had no intention of doing so, but he was pretty sure that both Val and Niall had noticed. Neither of them was stupid, and it might be time for Les to talk to them about it. He just wasn't sure how to do it. He didn't want Niall to feel like he was taking something away from him. He doubted Niall would feel that way, but that was still one of the reasons Les had decided to keep it to himself. That, and the fact that he wasn't that old yet.

He was only forty-four, which meant he wasn't thinking about retiring yet. It would be good to have someone help him with the accounts and the administrative part of the job, though, and he hoped that in time, Val would be that person.

Maybe he'd talk to them at dinner tonight. It was a family dinner, but they'd have all the time they needed to talk about whatever they wanted. Maybe Les could sneak in a little work.

He tried to imagine what Billy would say about that. He'd probably glare at Les until Les stopped, and just the thought of him doing that made Les smile.

Maybe it would be better to talk about work tomorrow.

Les quickly dried up, ignored his reflection in the mirror, and went to dress. Dinner wasn't anything special, so he wore jeans and a sweater. The evenings were still cool, even though spring had burst onto the scene. No one would care what he wore, anyway. He was meeting family, and he didn't need to impress them.

"Come on," he called out, listening for Hector. "I'll let you out before I leave."

He wasn't surprised there was no answer. The dog was lazier than he was, and that was saying something. If Hector had his way, he'd never leave his bed, or rather, Les's. At the moment, though, he wasn't in the bedroom. Les knew where he'd find him, so he headed to the guest room and leaned down to peek into the crate in the corner. Sure enough, Hector was huddled at the back of it. He opened an eye but didn't move, already trying to make Les feel guilty about leaving him alone.

Les sighed. "I don't have time for your dramatics. Come on. I need to leave the house in fifteen minutes, which means you just have the time to go outside."

Hector sighed as if Les had asked him to plow the backyard. He climbed out of the crate, stretched backward, then forward, and only when he was done followed Les out of the guest room and down the hallway. Now that he was out of the crate, he was getting excited about going out and bounded down the stairs.

Les shook his head, grinning like an idiot. He hadn't been sure it was a good idea for him to get a dog, but he hadn't been able to resist the boxer when he'd seen him at the rescue. He'd only been there to drop off a bunch of old blankets, but he'd come home with Hector.

He wouldn't have it any other way.

He let the dog out, then finished getting ready. There wasn't much else for him to do. He put some gel into his hair, pushed it away from his face so it didn't bother him, made sure he'd put on deodorant, then put his boots on. By the time he was ready, Hector was sitting in front of the door on the porch, waiting to be let in. When Les opened, Hector ignored him and made a beeline for the stairs.

"I'm not going back upstairs to say goodbye," Les warned him.

The damn dog was trying to make him feel guilty, but he needed to stand strong, something he'd never been able to do when it came to this dog.

Les went upstairs even though he'd told Hector he wouldn't. He found the dog curled up on his bed, looking like someone had killed his entire family. Les rolled his eyes, but he gave the dog a good scratch on top of the head, then kissed him there. "I'll be back soon."

The dog was a great actor. If Les hadn't known him, he might have been worried. This was what Hector did every time Les had to leave the house, though, so after one last scratch, Les went back downstairs. He grabbed his keys, wallet, and phone, ensured he had everything he might need, and finally left the house.

Luckily, nothing in Green Hill was far. He and his family were meeting at the diner, and while he could have been there in ten minutes if he'd walked, it was getting late, so he decided to take his truck. By the time he parked by the diner, he could see that at least one of his nephews was there. Flynn's car was a few spots down from his truck.

Les hurried toward the diner, looking around as soon as he stepped in. It wasn't late, which meant the place was hopping. Les waved at people and nodded as he walked between the crowded tables and booths. Glenda, one of the waitresses and owner of the diner, didn't try to stop him. He was a regular, and he'd done a lot of work at the diner, which meant they knew each other well.

He finally found the tables where his family had gathered toward the back of the diner. The first to notice him was Flynn, who grinned and waved him down. Les made a beeline for him, grinning when he saw he was the last one to arrive. Shona wasn't at the table, but her purse was there, which meant she couldn't be far.

Les slipped into the chair that had been kept empty for him, smiling at Flynn's mate, Jude, who was next to him. "Sorry I'm late."

"You're not," Jude reassured him.

Les leaned back against his chair and looked around the room. The men around it said hello, all smiling at him, and he smiled back.

This was his family, and even though sometimes, he felt out of place, he wouldn't have it any other way.

Thedric was finally free. He'd tried to leave right after dinner, but his mother had insisted that they needed to talk, which meant he'd been stuck there for another hour. He'd had to listen to both of his parents as they ranted about his brother and nephew, about how ungrateful they were and how their lives could be so much better if they just went along with what they wanted because they knew better.

Thedric had had to resist the urge to snort a few times.

He'd managed to do so only by biting the inside of his lip, and it felt a bit sore.

At least he was out of the house. His mother had told him to go to Leiana's room once he got home, but Thedric had no intention of doing anything like that. Leiana's room was hers, and he had no business being there for any reason.

He realized that for some people, what he and Leiana had would be odd. They'd gotten married because their parents had decided it was what they should do, and even though it had been twenty years, they'd never been intimate. They had no intention of changing that, but it wasn't like Thedric could tell his parents about their arrangement. They'd be appalled, and his father would probably push for him to do something like he'd said earlier.

Thedric shuddered in horror and quickly shimmered home. He did so from the spot just outside his parents' front door, shimmering to a similar spot on his own property. He relaxed once he was there, but his night wasn't over yet. He'd have to trudge through the too-big house until he reached his suite, and he wasn't looking forward to it. There were too many stairs, dammit.

The house had been a present from his and Leiana's parents when he and Leiana married. It was too big for two people, but he supposed they'd intended for him and Leiana to have many children. Even so, the house would have been too big. It had enough guest rooms to host a small army, which had been great when he and Leiana had realized they could never truly be husband and wife. They both needed their space, and they each had a suite of rooms on opposite sides of the house.

Sometimes, Thedric wondered if his parents knew. He wouldn't have been surprised if some of the servants had talked about it to their servants, but his parents had never shared rooms, either. He doubted they even liked each other, which explained the distance between them and the fact that they barely saw each other unless they had something to do as a couple.

The same could be said for Thedric and Leiana, but the reason they spent so little time together wasn't that they didn't like each other. It was because they had little in common. Both of them had their own lives, Thedric with his work, Leiana with her many friends and charity work. They didn't even see each other most nights, which was why he was surprised when, walking past the library, he noticed the light was on. Usually, Leiana was already in bed by the time he came home from his dinners with his parents.

Thedric hesitated. He'd been feeling things were about to change for a while now, and while he knew that wouldn't happen unless he made decisions and finally acted on them, Leiana was one of the reasons he hadn't yet. They needed to talk about their future and what Thedric's feelings about their lives would mean, but Thedric wasn't up for that kind of conversation. Still, it might be good to spend some time with Leiana. They'd become friends over the years, and she was an essential part of his life.

He knocked on the slightly open door, then pushed it open. Leiana was curled up in an armchair by the fireplace, her bare feet under her. She wore light-pink silk pajamas, and her blonde hair was braided and pulled over one of her shoulders. She had a book in her hand and a mug of something on the small table next to her. The fireplace was empty because it wasn't that cold anymore, but the area around it was still cozy, which was no doubt one of the reasons she'd chosen to spend the evening here.

She blinked up and smiled at Thedric even though she looked surprised to see him. "You're back from dinner with your parents," she said.

Thedric hesitated, then stepped into the room as he

nodded. "I am. Did you have a good evening?"

"I did, but I doubt I can say the same about you."

The gentle teasing made Thedric grin. "I don't think anyone who spent any time with my parents would call their evening good."

"You do realize you don't have to go, right? You're an adult, and you can say no."

That much was true. Until now, Thedric had clung to his parents because they were the only family he had left. Well, the only family who talked to him.

That had changed. Between talking to Damick again and Miko, Thedric felt like something was changing. It was as if something massive and buried deep inside of him had shifted, and while he didn't know what that something was, he didn't think it mattered.

But the result was that Thedric wasn't content with his life anymore. That was all he'd ever been. He couldn't be happy, but he'd never blamed Leiana for that. He doubted he made *her* happy, and that was because of the circumstances, not because of the kind of people they were.

Thedric had always thought this would be his life. When he'd married Leiana and they'd realized they couldn't be what the other needed, he'd been relieved. They'd been honest with each other, which wasn't something he'd thought could happen. He'd expected to have to lie to her, maybe go along with what she wanted. He'd thought she'd be like his mother, with a sharp tongue and no hesitation when it came to hurting someone with her words.

But Leiana was nothing like that. She was a sweet and gentle woman, and Thedric wished he could make her happy. He wished he could give her children, and she deserved so much more than he could give her.

But so did he.

He deserved more than a relationship that could never be

real. He deserved more than living this life, being content with not having to worry about anything but his job. Maybe he could find someone to be in a real relationship with? It wasn't something he'd ever dared hope for, but after seeing how his nephew had stood up to his parents, Thedric had started hoping.

And he wasn't sure he could stop now that he had.

"You know what would happen if I dared not go to our weekly dinners," he said.

Leiana wrinkled her nose. "Your mother would come here."

"Exactly. I only want to protect you from her."

Leiana's expression went soft. "You're not the only adult here. I can protect myself and might even be able to protect you."

Thedric almost told her he didn't need to be protected, but he wasn't sure that was true. Maybe everyone needed to be protected in some way, and even though he and Leiana weren't together, maybe she felt the way he did. They'd been in each other's lives for twenty years. They lived separate lives, but that didn't change the fact that they were married. It didn't have the same meaning it would have had if they'd married someone they were in love with, but it still meant something to Thedric.

He wasn't sure what any of this meant for his dreams of a happier future or if he could entangle his feelings, but maybe someone could help him do so.

After saying goodnight to Leiana, Thedric headed to his suite. As soon as he was in, he took off his jacket and tie and dumped them onto one of the armchairs by the fireplace. He grabbed his phone, his fingers trembling as he dialed his brother's number.

He'd dreamed of doing this for years, but it had been better for Damick and his family if Thedric stayed back. It had kept their parents' attention away from Damick, and Thedric had been happy to do this for his brother. He also hadn't known what to tell Damick, and he still didn't.

"Thedric?" Damick asked as he answered.

It took Thedric a moment to find the right words, and even when he did, he wasn't sure they *were* the right ones. "I want to see you."

"Why? Has something happened?"

"No. I just want to fix things between us." Thedric hoped it would be the first step to change his life, but even if Damick said no, at least Thedric was doing something. Only time would tell if that *something* was the right choice.

Les quickly hugged Billy, then Niall. "I'll see you tomorrow at work."

Niall groaned and rubbed his stomach. "I don't know about that. I feel like I'll need to be rolled out of bed tomorrow morning."

His mate elbowed him in the side. "I told you that you needed to slow down."

"But the food was delicious. If you don't want me to eat so much, you'll need to choose another place the next time we have dinner with the family."

Les shook his head, amused. It was always a delight watching his nephews with their mates. The love between them was so strong that Les could almost feel it, and it always brought a smile to his face. At the same time, it made him a little sad, and he could see that his niece felt the same way.

He wrapped an arm around Shona's shoulders and hugged her close. "Everything okay?" he whispered.

She smiled at him. "Yeah. I just might have eaten too much, like Niall."

"Runs in the family," Niall declared.

"Come on. I'll drive you home," Les told Shona.

"You don't have to," she protested, but it didn't last long.

She looked as tired as Les felt, and he could tell she couldn't wait to get home. The same went for him, so he guided her away from her brothers and the rest of the family. Everyone waved their goodbyes, and while Les loved all of them and enjoyed spending time with them, he sighed in relief when the level of noise dipped.

"They're a lot," Shona said as they climbed into Les's truck.

"Yeah, but they're family, so what can you do?"

"I don't think I'd want to change anything."

"They're perfect the way they are."

Even though sometimes Niall could be an idiot. Finding his mate had helped him mellow out a bit, and Les had noticed he was more responsible on the job. It was good to see, and he'd already thanked Billy several times over it. Billy always teased that meeting his mate changed a man and that Les would understand once he met his.

As far as Les was concerned, that wasn't about to happen.

They drove in silence for a little while. Les could tell something was on Shona's mind, but if he asked what was happening, she'd clam up. She'd always been the one sibling who held her heart close to her chest. Niall was the loud one, Flynn was the quiet one, and Shona was the one who felt things too strongly.

"I'm happy for them," she eventually said. "I mean, it's obvious that Billy and Jude make them happy, and I want that for them. I just can't help but wonder when it'll happen to me."

Les reached out and squeezed his niece's knee. "Eventually, it will. You're still young, so I wouldn't worry too much about that. I understand it can hurt to watch your brothers be so much in love and not have that in your life, though."

"What about you? Don't you want to meet your mate?"

Les hesitated. The relationship he had with his niece and nephews was odd. He'd been a surprise baby and was twenty years younger than his brother, their father. That meant there were only thirteen years of difference between him and Shona. He wasn't quite an authority figure for her and her brothers, but he also wasn't quite a friend. He'd always tried to be honest with them when he could.

"I'm not sure. I mean, who wouldn't want a love like the one your brothers have, right? But at the same time, I feel like maybe I'm too old to have that kind of relationship."

Shona snorted. "It's not like you're sixty. I wouldn't think you were too old to find your mate, even if you were. Look at Dad."

Regan was in his early sixties, and after losing the love of his life, he'd met Billy's mother and married her. They weren't mates but blissfully happy, so Les understood what Shona was talking about.

"I don't know if I could open my life to someone the way your father did," he confessed. "I've been alone for a long time, and I like things the way they are. I can only imagine what trying to add someone to my life would be like."

"It might be complicated, but it doesn't mean it wouldn't be worth it," Shona quietly pointed out. "I want to meet my mate."

"And I hope you'll meet them soon." She deserved it.

But her question made Les wonder. He loved his life. He owned his own construction business, a home he'd renovated with the help of his family, and he had a family who loved him. He had Hector, and all in all, his life was fulfilling.

But there was an empty spot in it. When he went home at night, there was no one to welcome him except for Hector. He loved his dog, but he couldn't help but imagine what it would be like if, now that he got home, there was someone on the couch waiting for him.

They would kiss, and Les's mate would ask how the evening had gone. He'd laugh when Les told him some of the things that had been said and done, and he'd let Les guide him toward the stairs so they could go to bed, dinner be damned.

Les shook his head. Maybe he wanted that, but that didn't mean he was actively looking for it. If his mate dropped into his lap tomorrow, he wouldn't push him away, but he doubted that would happen. His life had been the same for years, and while it was routine, it was familiar, and he liked it that way. He'd never been the kind of guy who needed to explore the world, be rich, or have hundreds of friends. His life might seem small to some people, but it was the way he liked it, and he didn't want it to change, at least not too much.

But Shona wanted a mate, and he hoped she'd find them.

After dropping her off at her apartment building, Les headed home. The silence in the car felt heavy, and it didn't get any better as he got closer to his house. His dream of having someone waiting for him on the couch was still in the back of his mind, and even though the house was empty, he couldn't help but hold his breath as he unlocked his front door and stepped in.

Hector was behind the door, his tail wagging so hard that his entire butt moved along with it. When Les crouched in front of him, Hector rushed into his arms, grinning at him with his doggy smile and trying to give him doggy kisses everywhere he could reach. Les didn't enjoy making out with his dog, so he tried to keep Hector away from his face while also showering him with affection.

But he couldn't help but peek sideways as he did so. The living room was dark and empty, just like he'd known it would be. There was no one waiting for him except Hector, and that wasn't going to change anytime soon.

After he let the dog out one last time, they both headed up

the stairs to get ready for bed. Hector was already in his spot when Les came out of the bathroom, and as Les settled into bed and Hector pressed against his legs, Les once again wondered what it would be like if he weren't alone.

Yes, his life was comfortable, and he liked it, but sometimes, he felt like he was sixty-four rather than forty-four. Hell, his brother had a more active social life than him, and he was twenty years older. Les might not be yearning for his mate, but surely, it wouldn't hurt to open his life just a bit. And if his mate happened to tumble into it when he did, Les wasn't about to send the man packing.

Chapter Two

Thedric stared at his reflection in the mirror. Was a suit too formal to meet his brother? But what else could he wear? He only ever wore suits, mostly because he didn't go anywhere but to work and his parents' house. He didn't think he had anything different in his closet, although he was willing to dig in and find out.

If only he had more time, he could go to the store and buy something. The problem was that he had no idea what he should buy. He was so used to suits that they felt natural to him, and he couldn't imagine himself in anything else. He didn't have to impress his brother, but he still wished to make a good impression, and he wasn't sure if the suit would lead to that or not.

He hesitated, then took off the tie and threw it onto the armchair by the mirror. He opened the shirt collar with trembling fingers, then looked at himself again.

It was odd to see himself without a tie. He wasn't sure he liked it, but he didn't have a lot of time left to get ready before he had to leave. He wasn't going to be late when his brother had agreed to talk to him so they could try to fix things between them.

It had been too long. They'd seen each other briefly when Miko needed help dealing with their parents, but there hadn't been time for Thedric and Damick to talk about what had happened between them. Thedric hadn't known what to say or how to apologize. He still didn't, but he'd do it anyway. He wanted his brother back, and he'd do whatever he needed in order to make that happen.

He knew that if he didn't make a decision, he would still be here in three hours, picking through his closet and wondering how he should dress. He buttoned his collar, grabbed the tie again, looped it around his neck, and quickly tied it. The suit and tie were him. There wasn't another Thedric, and maybe his brother should know that. They weren't the people they'd been twenty years ago, and it was no use trying to go back to that. Their relationship would have to be a brand new one, which, as far as Thedric was concerned, wasn't a bad thing. The relationship between him and his brother hadn't worked well twenty years ago, and if they didn't change it, it wouldn't work now, either.

He finished getting ready, re-braided his hair, then chose a watch and the right cologne. If he told himself he was getting ready for work, it was easier for him not to get too nervous, so he acted as if he was going to the office. It worked until he left his bedroom and made his way to the front of the house. For some reason, Leiana was in the entrance, poking at a vase of flowers on a table.

She turned when she heard him, a wide smile on her face. "You're ready," she said.

Thedric had told her he'd called his brother and that they were attempting to fix things between them. To his surprise, she'd been happy to hear that. She knew how much it had hurt Thedric to be without his brother for twenty years, and she wanted him to succeed.

"Are you meeting him at a restaurant?" she asked, looking him up and down.

"No. He gave me his address, and we're meeting at his home."

Leiana wrinkled her nose. "And you thought a suit and a tie were the right attire?"

A knot of panic grew in Thedric's chest. "It's too much? I

wasn't sure what to wear. I don't even know if I have something different."

Leiana raised her hands and came closer. "A suit is perfectly fine. You want to be yourself with your brother, and this is who you are."

Thedric nodded, but he wasn't quite sure that was the truth. He always wore suits because that was what his parents had taught him. He needed to be composed and look perfect and in control, and that was what he'd aimed for every day of his life. Wearing a suit made sense when he went to work and even when he met his parents, but most people didn't wear suits at home.

There was no time for him to change, though.

He looked at himself and smoothed down his suit jacket. "I'm going to be late if I waste more time."

Leiana hesitated, then gently touched Thedric's shoulder. "Be yourself. You're a sweet and gentle man, and I'm sure your brother will see that. Both of you come from the same parents, so he knows what they're like. You helped him with his son, and I'm sure he wouldn't have agreed to talk to you if he didn't want to fix things, too. I know you're nervous, and I'm sure he is, too. Just remember who you are."

Thedric frowned. "What do you mean?"

"The two of you are brothers. That's something that will never change, but it doesn't mean you have to have a relationship. The fact that both of you want one is good, and I hope you won't allow your parents to ruin it."

"I'm not letting them ruin anything ever again," Thedric said.

He was convinced of that, even though he didn't know what it would mean. He'd find out soon enough. He was sure his parents would eventually discover he'd met with his brother, and when they did, there would be hell to pay.

He was ready to do exactly that.

He kissed Leiana's cheek. "I'll see you later."

"I'm not going anywhere. I'm happy for you, Thedric."

Thedric nodded and stepped out of the door. He stepped into the shimmering spot, gave his wife one last glance, then shimmered away, thinking of his brother.

He landed next to a small house. Well, it was small compared to his, but it was definitely big enough for a family of three. A wide porch ran around it, cluttered with a bench, several pairs of boots, and umbrellas. There was a potted plant next to the front door, and the lights were on inside. He could hear people talking, and he swallowed.

This was it.

The door opened before Thedric could climb the porch steps. His brother stood there, squinting at him, and Thedric held his breath, unsure what to say.

"You're here," Damick said.

Thedric stopped keeping himself in check. He climbed the porch steps two by two, then dragged his brother in for a hug. Damick squeaked, but his arms wrapped around Thedric, and they stood in each other's arms for the first time in years. It had been more than twenty years since their last hug. Their parents had scolded them for any signs of affection when they were children because they shouldn't show emotions, and it was so ingrained in Thedric that he wasn't sure what had gotten into him. He couldn't let go of his brother, and Damick seemed to understand that. He was murmuring things in Thedric's ear and gently rubbing his back.

He'd always been more open and less stiff than Thedric, and that hadn't changed.

"I'm happy to see you," Damick said as he leaned back.

Thedric nodded. He wasn't sure he could say anything without crying. He needed to get himself under control, so he took a step back, shaking himself.

"It's *really* good to see you," Damick repeated.

"It is," Thedric croaked.

It was as if nothing had changed between them. The last twenty years didn't feel like they'd happened. Thedric felt as close to his brother as he had when they were children, and he prayed Damick felt the same.

"Why don't you come in? We can sit on the couch and talk for a bit, but I have a birthday party to go to in a while."

Thedric frowned. He'd hoped he and his brother would have many hours to be together, but he understood that Damick had other people in his life. "I can go and come back tomorrow or the day after that." He didn't want his brother to feel like he needed to change his plans because of him.

But Damick shook his head as he guided Thedric into the house. "There's no need for that. I'm ready to go whenever Klotild is, and it's just a birthday party for a friend." He cocked his head. "Actually, you should come."

"Why?"

"Why not? These people are family, and so are you. If you're going to be in my life, you'll meet them eventually, and the same goes for Klotild and Miko. You need to be truly part of our lives. I want you to be."

Thedric wasn't sure that going to a birthday party for a stranger was a good idea, but how could he say no to his brother?

Les opened his front door to find what appeared to be his entire family standing on the porch. He blinked, then quickly tried to remember if he knew anything about whatever was happening. He couldn't remember anyone telling him they were coming over.

"What's going on?" he asked Niall, who seemingly had been the one to knock.

Niall raised his hands. "Don't blame me. It wasn't my

idea."

Shona pushed past him. She carried two plastic bags heavy with something, and Les tried to take them from her, but she glared at him. "Let's start. We don't have a lot of time."

"What's going on?" Les asked again as everyone filed into the house.

Hector, who'd been sleeping on his pillow in the living room, clearly wasn't sure what to make of so many people in his house. He stared from the living room door, his body vibrating. Les wanted answers, too, so he understood where Hector was coming from.

"I'm not sure how it started," Billy explained as he walked in with Jude. "We were talking about you and how it was your birthday and how we knew you wouldn't organize anything."

Les groaned. "There's a reason I don't do anything for my birthday." Mostly, it was because it was kind of sad to celebrate it on his own. What was he supposed to do? Get a cake for him and Hector and buy himself a gift? He sometimes celebrated with his family over dinner, but they hadn't talked about it, so he hadn't planned anything special for today. He hadn't even been sure anyone remembered it was his birthday, and that was fine with him.

Clearly, it wasn't with Shona.

Jude smiled gently. "We just want to celebrate with you."

"And you decided to invade my home?"

"That was Shona's idea. Just to make sure you're ready for it, we won't be the only ones here tonight. She invited more people."

Les groaned. He hadn't expected this and wasn't sure what to make of it. There was no saying no to this birthday party, though. Everyone was here, and Les didn't want them to be disappointed.

He supposed that, for once, he'd have a birthday party.

His entire family was here, including Regan and his wife. The group took over the house in minutes, and Les wasn't quite sure what to do with himself. He did his best to stay out of the way and wondered if he needed to change. He had on jeans and a sweater, which should be fine for a home birthday party, but he didn't know what Shona had in mind.

"I tried to stop her," Regan said, sounding apologetic.

The two of them huddled in the living room, far away from the proceedings. The couch was being moved to the side, and Shona was directing everyone as if she were a colonel or something like that.

"It's fine," Les reassured his brother.

Regan didn't look convinced. "I know you don't celebrate your birthday and that you don't like crowds."

"This isn't a crowd."

"Not yet," Regan muttered.

Les was afraid to ask. Billy and Jude had mentioned that Shona had invited people, but they hadn't said how many. Hopefully, Shona would have known only to invite people related to the family. Some would be strangers to Les but not to the others in the room, so it would be fine.

Hopefully.

"How are things going?" he asked his brother in an attempt to distract himself from what was about to happen.

Regan beamed. "The last time I was this happy was when Liane was alive."

"I'm glad you found Maris."

And Les really was. He'd been there when his brother lost his first wife. It had almost destroyed Regan. The only reason he hadn't given in to the pain and sadness was that he'd had three children to take care of. He'd carried on for them, but along the way, he'd healed, and he was happy again. He had everything he deserved.

But it made Les wonder about himself. He hadn't had even

one love, let alone two. He wasn't sure it was in the cards for him, and it made him kind of sad, especially as he looked around. Regan had a besotted expression as he watched his wife, Maris, talk with Shona. Billy and Niall were bickering over something by the window while Flynn and Jude were working together, following Shona's orders. Their love shone, and Les wondered if he would ever have that.

What was happening to him? He didn't use to be like this, obsessing over having a partner. He was fine on his own and didn't feel lonely, even though he sometimes felt alone. When that happened, he spent time with his family, like tonight.

He was okay with his life. He didn't need anyone, but that didn't mean he didn't *want* someone.

A knock on the door made him turn toward his brother. Regan grinned and shrugged while Shona freaked out on the other side of the room.

"It's early," she cried out.

"I'll see who it is," Jude reassured her before disappearing into the entrance. He came back with a bunch of people Les didn't know well but had met before. He was pretty sure one of them was Jude's brother, and unless he was wrong, the man next to Nestor was his mate.

Somehow, all of these people were related to Les, even though he barely knew them. They were family, even though they weren't close, but that was fine with Les. One could never have enough family if it was a good one, and the people around him were good people. Maybe this would be an opportunity for Les to get to know them. It was more than he'd expected for his birthday, and he found himself smiling.

Even though he hadn't planned for a birthday party and should probably be annoyed at the way Shona had taken over, he couldn't be. These people were here to celebrate him and because they loved him, and to him, that meant everything.

Another knock sent Hector flying toward the entrance. By now, he'd understood that people kept coming, and he had to be a bit frightened. He'd always been wary of strangers, so while someone else went to answer, Les grabbed him and carried him upstairs. He didn't want to take the dog away from the party, but it wasn't like Hector understood, and it would be easier for him to be up here and relax. That way, he wouldn't have to deal with so many people he didn't know.

By the time Les had settled Hector into his crate and spent a bit of time cuddling him, half an hour had passed. He'd heard more knocks on the door, so he knew there would be a crowd, but as he descended the stairs, he was stunned by the sheer number of people hanging around his living and dining rooms. There were more people in the kitchen, and everyone seemed to be having fun. Les didn't recognize most of them, but that didn't matter. He looked around, and his chest swelled with affection. Somehow, these people were all part of his family and were here for him.

A blond man he didn't know caught his eye. He looked out of place, standing against the wall, wearing a suit and a tie. He held himself stiffly as he talked to another blond man who looked like him, which made Les think they were related. The second man was wearing jeans and a sweater, though, and he looked much more at ease. Both of them had pointed ears, which told Les they were Nix.

He tried to think. Who was a Nix in his family? The only people he could think of were Miko and Farley, who were friends with Nestor, Jude's brother, and since Jude was mated to Les's nephew, it made him and them family. Maybe these two guys were related to them. It would make sense, but while Les was tempted to go over and introduce himself, something held him back.

Maybe he'd spend some time watching the man with the suit. For some reason, he fascinated Les, and that wasn't something Les often felt. He could find out who the guy was later. For now, he was more than happy to stare at him and enjoy the view.

Standing alone against the living room wall, Thedric had no idea why he was here. Hell, he didn't have any idea of *where* he was. When he'd agreed to come to the birthday party with his brother, Damick had dragged him out of the house. He'd explained who was organizing the party, but Thedric had lost track as they walked, and now, as he looked around, he only recognized a few people.

His brother was in the room, along with his mate. Thedric had seen Miko, his mate, and Farley, Miko's best friend. Thedric hadn't known him until today, but Miko had seemed excited to introduce them and to see Thedric there. He'd hugged Thedric in a way Thedric hadn't expected, and he had to work hard on not crying. He was overwhelmed, and he wouldn't have it any other way.

Well, he wished he didn't have so many people he didn't know around, but from what he could see, his brother knew all of them, and they seemed almost like a family. That wasn't something he and Damick had growing up, and it was good to see that he'd created his own family after their parents had decided to kick him out of their lives. All in all, Damick had built himself a good life. He had a mate, a son, and he was happy. His life was rich with people, something Thedric couldn't say about his.

"I know this is a lot," Damick said, coming closer.

Thedric plastered a smile on his face. "It's fine."

Damick laughed. "You look like a deer in headlights, but it's okay. I promise. These people are all family in one way or another, and they'll accept you because you're here."

"I'm sure they're wondering who I am."

"I have no doubt, and some of them will come up to you and introduce themselves eventually, but I don't want you to worry. You belong here, just like I do."

Thedric pressed his lips together. "Why?"

"You're my brother."

Thedric hadn't thought it would be that easy. He'd believed he and Damick would talk, then retreat to their homes to think about everything. He'd thought it would take them a lot more time to feel comfortable with each other and that they'd have to talk things through several times.

He had no doubt they would. What their parents had done to both of them had left scars, and if they wanted those scars to heal, they'd need to talk things out. Damick didn't seem in a rush to do so, though, and Thedric wasn't, either. He was fine settling back into his relationship with his brother since Damick seemed to have accepted him into his life as if he'd never left. Everything else, every complication, could be dealt with later.

"Thank you," he said, his voice trembling.

"You're family," Damick repeated, and Thedric believed him.

He'd never felt this way. Technically, he, Damick, and their parents had been a family. They'd never felt like one, at least not in the way this family felt. Things had always been tense and stiff, as if more than a family, they were coworkers who didn't even like each other. These people were entirely different. They loved each other and had welcomed Thedric without even asking who he was. Thedric might not know how to deal with it, but he didn't have to find out right now.

He stuck close to his brother, feeling safe with Damick even though they hadn't talked much in twenty years. Eventually, though, someone called out to Damick, and he left Thedric behind. Thedric didn't miss how he hesitated, so he waved at his brother to talk to his friend. "I'll be fine," he promised.

And he was, mostly.

He was a little lost as he looked around, but he straightened his back and squared his shoulders. He might not know how to behave when it came to family, but he owned a successful company and had created an app that most people in the room probably had on their phones. He was used to meeting people he didn't know and making a good impression, so maybe he had to think of the people around him as work opportunities. It didn't feel quite right, but it was better than cowering in a corner for the rest of the evening.

He moved away from the wall and headed toward a long table against the wall that had been set up with drinks and food. Several people smiled at him, and he nodded back, even though he had no idea who they were. Thankfully, no one tried talking to him, and he felt slightly better by the time he had a drink and retreated toward his corner of the room.

This was nothing like the parties his parents organized every so often. Even if he stood in the corner the entire evening, he'd be fine.

Something bumped against his leg, and he looked down to see a massive dog sitting next to him. More than a dog, it looked like a small horse, and Thedric took a step back, slightly horrified. The dog sat there, his head cocked, staring at Thedric. Was he thinking about how to eat Thedric? Surely not. This was a dog, not a hellhound, but Thedric had never had a pet. He had no idea how to behave and wasn't sure that finding out tonight was the best idea.

"Good dog," he said, forcing a smile on his lips.

For some reason, the dog seemed to be delighted by those words. He leaned against Thedric's leg, and there was nowhere for Thedric to go. He was stuck between the dog and the wall. He looked around for his brother, hoping Damick could help.

"Not a fan of dogs?" a voice asked.

It wasn't Damick, but if the man was going to help, Thedric was fine with whoever it was. He looked up even though he wasn't sure it was a good idea to move his gaze away from the dog. His gaze locked with the gaze of the man who'd been talking to him, and Thedric couldn't look away.

How could he have when his mate was standing in front of him?

He opened his mouth, but nothing came out. The man stared at him for a moment, then shrugged and turned his attention to the dog. He was gorgeous, with broad shoulders, brown hair and eyes, and a hint of stubble on his cheeks. He looked at ease, which told Thedric he was part of the core family who organized this party tonight. Either that, or he enjoyed being with so many people he barely knew, which Thedric supposed was possible.

The man was talking to the dog. "I should probably put you upstairs with Hector. I can't have you scaring pretty men all night."

It took Thedric a moment to realize the man was talking about him. He thought Thedric was pretty.

Thedric supposed it was a good thing, since they were mates.

The man hadn't reacted to Thedric's presence, so he probably wasn't a shifter. Considering the mix of Nix, shifters, and humans around the room, it was easy to guess he was human. He wouldn't know he was Thedric's mate until Thedric told him, but Thedric wasn't sure he could make his mouth work at the moment. He could only stare at the man who was supposed to be his for the rest of their lives.

"I'm Thedric," he croaked.

His mate smiled. "Les."

"It's a pleasure to meet you, Les."

It really was. Thedric hadn't thought this would happen to him. He'd been happy for Miko and Damick, but he'd also been jealous. He'd wanted what they had with their mates, but it had felt like a pointless dream. No one could choose when they met their mate, and clearly, Thedric's time hadn't come yet.

Except that it had. Fate didn't make mistakes, as far as Thedric was concerned. He didn't care that his parents didn't believe in mates. They felt that way because when Damick had met his mate and had been strong enough to stand up to them, it had taken away the control they had over him.

And now, they were about to lose control over Thedric, too.

Thedric couldn't remember being as happy as he was at the moment, but he was also really freaking confused.

Les had kept an eye on the Nix he'd noticed earlier, so it hadn't been hard to see that the man was out of place, and not only because of the suit. He'd stuck close to the other Nix the entire evening, which reinforced the feeling that they were related. As soon as Les had been able to, he'd talked to Miko, who'd confirmed that the man was his uncle. That explained why the man was here, and Les had decided to try to make him feel more at home. In a way, they were family, and even if the man wasn't close to his brother and nephew, he and Les would probably see each other again during family celebrations.

Duke had given Les the perfect excuse. Flynn had been apologetic when he told Les he'd brought the dog, but Duke was much better with strangers and crowds than Hector. Les had checked up on him several times during the evening, and he'd always found him sitting at someone's feet, usually begging for food with his soulful eyes. Everyone had been fine with him, but when he sat at Thedric's feet, Les had decided to intervene. Thedric had seemed uncomfortable with the dog, which was understandable when someone wasn't used to animals. Duke was massive, and he could appear scary to people who didn't know him. But for some reason, Thedric still seemed frozen. He was staring at Les with wide eyes, and he'd only been able to croak his name out.

"Oh God, did he do something?" Flynn asked as he rushed to Les's side.

"Not that I'm aware of. I just think Thedric isn't used to dogs," Les explained, gesturing at the man next to him.

Flynn grabbed the dog's collar and pulled him away. "Sorry about that. He's a teddy bear, so you don't have to worry about him hurting you. He's just been begging for food as if I didn't feed him before leaving the house."

Thedric seemed to realize Flynn was talking to him and came to life. He turned his attention fully to Flynn and nodded. "Of course. I apologize."

"You don't have anything to apologize for. I do, and I'm really sorry."

Thedric smiled. "Let's agree that neither of us did anything wrong. Your dog is interesting."

Flynn laughed. "You meant massive and kind of scary."

"I have to admit I didn't expect dogs to come in such big forms. I'm not used to animals."

"Well, if you ever want to get used to them, Duke is a perfect choice. I promise that he'd never hurt a fly. He's big, but he doesn't didn't have the energy to do more than sleep and beg for food."

Thedric chuckled.

He was charming like this, a completely different man than Les had observed before. Les had been watching him since he'd first noticed him, and Thedric had been so obviously out of place that it almost hurt. His suit and the way he behaved told Les he probably had a lot of money, which had made him wonder what Thedric was doing here. The fact that they were somewhat related explained that, but surely Thedric had better things to do than to be here this evening. From the look of him, he should be at a posh party, sipping champagne and eating fish eggs, or whatever people ate at posh parties. Instead, he had to make do with beer and pizza.

"I'm Flynn," Flynn said, offering Thedric's hand.

Thedric shook it eagerly. "Thedric."

"Since you're a Nix, you must be somehow related to Miko or Farley."

"I'm Miko's uncle. My brother Damick invited me." Thedric looked around. "I hope it's not a problem. I don't know whose birthday it is, and I wasn't supposed to be here."

Les chuckled. "Don't worry about it. I'm happy to have you here."

Thedric stared. "It's *your* birthday?"

"It is, and this is my home. You're welcome to stay for as long as you want." The longer he stayed, the happier Les would be. He didn't understand why he was so fascinated by Thedric, but he didn't need a reason to give in to that feeling. He was curious and wouldn't find out anything about Thedric if he didn't talk to the man.

But for some reason, Thedric had tensed again. He nodded curtly. "Well, happy birthday, Les."

"Thank you."

"I'm afraid I didn't get you a gift. It was extremely rude of me, as was inviting myself without asking you first."

Les exchanged a glance with Flynn. His nephew appeared as puzzled as he felt, and he was desperate to keep Thedric here, but he could feel Thedric was about to run.

"I didn't expect this party, so I wasn't expecting gifts. Don't worry about it."

But Thedric shook his head. "I'll get you something. I can have it delivered here tomorrow."

"I promise you it's fine." But it was clear this was important to Thedric. "But if you want to get me something, feel free to do so. I won't say no to a gift."

Thedric looked around, spotted a small table, and leaned over to put down his glass. "I'm afraid I have to go, but it was nice meeting you."

"You don't have to leave."

"I wasn't supposed to attend this party and need to go home. I'm sure I'll see you soon, though."

Before Les could insist he stay or ask for his number, he stepped away. He vanished into the crowd, and since Les didn't want him to think he was a creep, he stayed where he was instead of trying to follow.

"That was weird," Flynn said as he let go of Duke's collar.

Duke leaned against Flynn's leg, looking like he might be about to fall asleep, even with the noise around him.

"I have a feeling that Thedric is a weird kind of guy," Les said slowly.

"And he's part of our family now." Eventually, they'd see each other again. If they didn't, Les could always find Miko or his father and ask about Thedric.

Flynn was staring, and when he saw he'd gotten Les's attention, he smiled. "Something's got you all knotted up."

"I'm not sure what it is about Thedric, but I wanted him to stay longer."

Flynn's eyes widened. "Oh, *that* kind of something. You like him?"

"I don't know yet." Because Les didn't know Thedric. He just knew that the man looked too perfect and that he wanted to ruffle his feathers, maybe see how beautiful he was when he lost his composure. Les had seen a hint of it when they'd met a few minutes ago, but he knew there was more to the man.

And he wanted to find out what that more was.

"Where's Les?" Shona suddenly asked, clapping her hands to get everyone's attention.

Les groaned and wondered if he could hide behind Duke. The dog was big enough for him to try, but before he could, Shona saw him.

She beamed. "There you are. It's time for cake." She looked around the room, her eyes getting narrower as she did so. "And everyone is going to sing happy birthday."

Several people protested, but a glare from her was enough to get them to agree. Les didn't really want everyone to sing happy birthday to him because he knew that at least a few people in the room couldn't carry a tune to save their lives, but this was family, too. He had no doubt he'd have to sing happy birthday to whoever had a birthday next. It was only fair that they sang to him, no matter how embarrassing it was for everyone involved.

Shona disappeared into the kitchen to get the cake, and when Les turned back to Flynn, it was to find his nephew still staring. "What?"

Flynn shook his head. "Nothing. I just don't think I've ever seen you interested in anyone the way you're interested in Thedric."

He wasn't wrong. "I guess I want to know what makes him tick. He looks so perfectly put together that I can't help but wonder how much fun it would be to find the man under the suit."

And that was all there was to it. It had to be.

Chapter Three

When Thedric was confused or lost, there was one thing that always made him feel better. So the day after meeting his mate, he decided to do just that and went to work.

Being in his office gave him a sense of peace. Here, he could escape from his parents and keep them away, because while they were happy he earned so much money with his apps, they thought it was beneath him to work on something like that. His father worked at a bank, and he'd expected Thedric to do the same. He'd been disappointed when Thedric had gone another way, but Thedric was delighted to have even more space to put between them. He'd taken advantage of that several times, knowing his parents thought it was beneath them to come to the office, especially after he'd started hiring humans, shifters, and other supernatural creatures. They'd expected him to only work with Nix, but Thedric had ignored their feelings over that. This was his business, and he'd make his own decisions.

Except that right now, he wasn't making any decision. Instead, he was pacing his office after having taken off his suit jacket and tie. If anyone could see him, they'd be able to tell something was wrong. His assistant had given him a strange look when he'd walked past her earlier on his way to his office, and she hadn't tried knocking on his door, even though he was sure there was work to do and meetings to attend. He was grateful for the respite, but he also felt guilty because since he was here, he should be working.

Had he done the right thing, leaving the birthday party last night? He hadn't been sure yesterday, and he still wasn't. But he'd been overwhelmed, and it felt like the best thing to do. He knew where to find Les, and he might have to knock on Les's door eventually, but first, he needed to wrap his mind around what had happened and make decisions.

He was married. Even though he hadn't wanted to marry Leiana and their marriage was a sham, they'd still gone through with the ceremony and everything. She was his wife, and it had meant something for twenty years, albeit not what it would have meant to someone else. Thedric loved her as a friend and knew what the divorce would mean for both of them. That didn't mean he wasn't planning on exploring that option, but they had to talk things out and plan accordingly. He hadn't even told her he'd met his mate yet, though, and he was going to have to do that.

He flopped down in his chair behind his desk and grabbed a notepad and a pen. Since he didn't know where to start, making a list would help. He traced a line down the page, then on one side of it, wrote *pros*, and on the other side, *cons*.

He stared at the page for a moment. Did he have to do this? Were there really pros and cons to meeting his mate?

Thedric pushed the piece of paper away, angry with himself. This wasn't a business decision he could make this way. This was meeting his mate, changing his life, and he couldn't view it as anything else. No one would expect him to, and he shouldn't, either. Besides, he already knew what he wanted, didn't he?

Thedric had always told himself that his marriage with Leiana wasn't a problem because neither of them had met their mate. In a way, he believed that both of them had tried to avoid meeting new people as much as possible since they'd gotten married because they hadn't wanted to deal with the consequences of what would happen if they met their mate. He'd focused on his work because there was nothing else for him to focus on, but now, there was no avoiding his mate. Even when they weren't together, he couldn't stop thinking about Les, and that wasn't going to change.

A knock on the door made him jump. He hadn't told his assistant not to bother him, but he'd thought she understood she needed to stay away. "Yes?"

The door cracked open, and she peered in. "I apologize, sir, but I have someone here that says he's your nephew."

Thedric shot to his feet. "Miko is here?"

She appeared relieved. "Along with a friend. Is it okay if I let them in?"

"Of course." Thedric welcomed the distraction. Maybe by the time Miko and Farley left, he'd feel more settled and would be able to make a decision when it came to Les.

She retreated, and a few seconds later, the door opened again. Miko peeked in, his blue hair wild around his face. He grinned when he saw Thedric, and Thedric walked around his desk, weirdly happy to see his nephew.

They'd never had a relationship. Thedric had kept an eye on his brother, so he'd known Damick had a child, but he hadn't met Miko until recently. Miko was already nineteen, and Thedric had missed so much of his life. He wanted to fix that, and while there was no going back, he could see them becoming close in the future.

Or at least, he hoped they would.

"I hope we're not bothering you," Miko said as he walked toward Thedric, Farley right behind him.

Farley's eyes were wide as he looked out the massive windows at the skyscrapers around them. "You work here every day?" he asked.

Thedric chuckled. "No. I enjoy working from home, too, and I often do so. And don't worry, you're not bothering me. Why don't you sit down? Do you want something to drink or eat?"

To Thedric's surprise, Miko stopped in front of him and hugged him. It was quick and not very strong, but it was more than Thedric had expected, and he felt like his heart might burst open. He wanted a relationship with Miko, but he hadn't been sure Miko wanted one with him. Now, he was.

Miko sat and peered at Thedric. "What happened last night? We were worried when you disappeared."

Thedric grimaced and led the way toward the corner of the room where several couches and a coffee table had been placed. "I apologize."

"You don't have to. We just wondered if something had happened. I wasn't sure what to think when Dad invited you to come, but I thought it would be fun. I didn't realize that it might not be good for you since you didn't know anyone there."

They sat, and Thedric fiddled with his cufflink. He wasn't sure how much to tell Miko and Farley. They weren't friends, and he wasn't sure becoming their friend was a good idea considering the age difference, but they were family. Family advised you, right? And not in the way his parents always had, trying to force him into one direction or another.

Thedric had thought about talking to his brother about this, but he felt there was too much unsaid between them to be able to at the moment. He supposed the same could be said about Miko, but his nephew was here, and Miko could tell something was wrong.

Thedric forced a smile on his face. "Why don't we order lunch?"

Miko arched a brow but didn't call Thedric out on the distraction. Instead, he and Farley leaned closer, and the three of them decided what they wanted to eat together, then placed an order. Once that was done, Miko's attention went back to the problem he'd sensed.

"You don't have to tell us anything, but we're family," he

said.

Thedric sighed. This was the best way to get him to talk, and while he doubted Miko knew that, he'd nailed it anyway. "I didn't leave because I wasn't comfortable. I left because I met someone, and I was overwhelmed."

Farley's eyes went wide again. "It was Les, wasn't it? I saw the two of you talking."

Thedric nodded. "It was. I didn't realize it was his birthday until we started talking." He swallowed and licked his lips. He'd never said these words to anyone, and he couldn't believe his nephew was the first person he'd say them to. "But as soon as I saw him, I could tell he was my mate."

There was a moment of silence as if all the sound had been sucked from the room. Farley and Miko stared, and Thedric braced himself for what he knew was coming. They'd be surprised and would want to talk about what had happened, which was one of the reasons he hesitated to tell them. He wasn't sure there was anything to say.

But it felt good to lift this weight off his shoulders. Now he only had to hope that Miko and Farley would have an idea of what he should do next.

Les's phone kept vibrating. At first, he'd checked every time because it could be someone contacting him for a job, but when he'd realized it was the family group text, he'd stopped. Whatever the family was talking about wasn't his problem while he was at work.

But it was lunchtime, and his fingers were itching to check. The vibrating hadn't stopped. If anything, it had gotten worse, and he'd started to suspect it was because he was ignoring the texts. For some reason, his family wanted to talk to him, and they clearly wouldn't stop trying until he gave them something.

The problem was that he wasn't sure he had anything to give.

He had no doubt the many texts had something to do with Thedric. A few people had mentioned him last night after he'd left, and even though Les had wanted to demand they tell him everything they knew about the man, he hadn't even mentioned him. He didn't know what to make of what had happened with Thedric or of the man himself. Les couldn't remember the last time he'd been so drawn to someone, and he didn't fully understand it.

But he hadn't missed the way both Val and Niall kept peering at him as they worked. He told them to focus on the job a few times, but he was pretty sure something was going to happen if they didn't get what they wanted. They were distracted, and he'd do whatever he could to make sure that stopped. Their job could be dangerous, and he didn't want anyone to get hurt.

He lowered his hammer and glared at the two, who were painting the wall on the other side of the room. "I can feel you staring at me."

"We weren't staring," Niall quickly said.

"Much," Val added. "We were just wondering about last night."

Les sighed, set down the hammer, and turned to face the two. His phone vibrated in his jeans again, and it caused him to glare. "Is that what all these messages are about? Last night?"

Val grimaced. "Pretty much. They've been texting us, too, demanding we ask for answers."

"What do you want to know?" Les's life was pretty much an open book. He wasn't sure he was ready to talk about Thedric, but it looked like he would have to. It was either tell Niall and Val about Thedric or have half his family take over the worksite and not leave him alone until he gave them what they wanted.

"We saw you talking to someone."

Les nodded. "I talked to many people last night."

"We saw you talking to a hot guy," Niall interjected. Val glared at him, but Niall didn't seem to care. "Who was it?"

"His name is Thedric. I'm not sure how he ended up at my birthday party since I'd never met him before, but I'm pretty sure he's related to one of the Nix in the family."

Niall nodded. "Makes sense. What did the two of you talk about? Are you going to see him again? Because let me tell you, if I weren't happily mated, *I'd* want to see him again."

"Stop sticking your nose where it doesn't belong, or I'll tell Billy what you just said," Les threatened.

Niall raised his hands, flicking paint over his t-shirt. "I'm just saying. I know you haven't dated anyone in a while, and the guy didn't look like he'd be a bad option."

"I don't think he would be, but something spooked him. That's why he left so quickly." Les would give pretty much anything to find out what had spooked Thedric, but it wasn't a question these two could answer. "Are you done with the questions?"

Val hesitated. "We are, but you know how the family is."

"Unfortunately, I do."

"We just want you to be happy. Everyone does. That's why we were excited to see you talking to a guy and hope you got his number."

"Unfortunately, I didn't have time. He left before I could."

Niall grimaced. "But I'm sure we can find a way to get him to talk to you again. Who did you say he was?"

"I only know that his name is Thedric. I'm pretty sure he's related to Miko, but I wouldn't swear on it."

"We can get you his number regardless. If he's who you want, everyone will support you."

Les rubbed his face, hoping he wasn't getting it dirty. He

understood where his family was coming from, and he was even grateful for how interested they were in his life and how important it was to them for him to be happy. Still, he didn't want them sticking their noses into this situation.

It would be easier to get someone to give him Thedric's number, but he needed to do this on his own. If he wanted Thedric's number, he could go to Miko and talk to him. They'd never spoken before, but Miko had been present at Les's birthday party, so he had to know who Les was. Les was sure they could find a way to communicate, and hopefully, he'd be able to gently prod and find out more about Thedric.

"I'll be fine," he insisted. "And you need to get back to work. I don't want to talk about Thedric anymore."

"Are you sure?" Val sounded worried, and while Les knew both he and Niall would listen if he needed to rant or had anything to say about Thedric, he wasn't about to do so. "I'm sure," he confirmed. "I don't need to talk to anyone, so get back to work."

Niall gave Les a little salute, then turned back to the wall. Val stared for a bit longer, but when Les nodded at him, he went back to work.

"Are you sure there's nothing between you and Thedric?" Niall asked a few minutes later.

Les groaned. "We just talked about this. I don't know the man, and there's nothing between us."

"I wouldn't be too sure about that."

"What are you talking about?" If this was a way for Niall to avoid getting back to work, Les was going to beat his ass.

When Niall turned toward Les, he was grinning like an idiot. "Because he just appeared in the front yard."

Les stared for a moment, wondering if he'd heard that right. "In *this* front yard?"

Niall's smile widened, something Les hadn't thought possible. "Yep. He's out there looking a bit lost. Do you want me to go to him?"

Les glared. "Don't you dare leave this room until you're done painting it. I'll go see what he wants." Les wouldn't have let anyone else do so in his place. There was no way Thedric was here to see anyone but him.

Right?

He wasn't sure, but he hoped, even though he didn't understand why. He didn't understand much of anything when it came to the situation between him and Thedric, but he supposed he was about to find out if something was going on between them.

Les looked down at himself. He'd been working, which meant he wasn't in the best state to meet Thedric, who he suspected was once again wearing an expensive suit and a tie. He tried brushing off some of the dirt and dust, but there was little he could do about the fact that he'd been working for hours and smelled like it. Hopefully, Thedric liked his men a bit rough because, at the moment, that was all Les could give him.

But if there was ever to be anything between them, Thedric would need to see Les in all of his aspects, including this one. They might as well get it out of the way, and Les hoped it wouldn't be a deterrent. He wanted to find out why Thedric was here, but even more so, he wanted to find out what Thedric's lips felt like and what his mouth tasted like.

Hopefully, he was about to.

Thedric stared at the house in front of him. It wasn't where Les lived, but he supposed it made sense. At this time of day, Les was at work like most people, which was why Thedric was starting to wonder if it was a good idea for him to do this.

He'd listened to Miko and Farley, and maybe he shouldn't have. When he'd explained the situation to them after shocking them into silence, they'd immediately tried to help. It was good to see they were happy for him, but Thedric suspected they would meddle if he didn't give in and go talk to Les. They knew Les better than he did, after all.

Hence he was here. He'd promised Miko he would at least try reaching out, but also that he'd tell Les they were mates. Miko wasn't wrong when he said that was only right. Humans didn't have mates, but when they happened to be a shifter or a Nix's mate, they deserved to know. It wouldn't be fair for Thedric to keep that kind of information to himself, although he should probably have thought better about when and where to tell Les.

He looked around. It would be better for him to leave, maybe try to get Les's phone number from someone. He had no doubt Miko would get it for him if he didn't have it himself. Thedric had been eager to see Les again, but he could see how this was the wrong move.

"Thedric?" a voice asked from the house.

While Thedric had been overthinking the situation, Les had noticed him. He was standing on the porch by the open door, a frown on his face as he stared.

Dammit. There was no getting out of this now. Thedric supposed he could find an excuse, but what would explain his presence here? Now that he thought about it, Les would probably feel he was a stalker. They barely knew each other, yet Thedric had shimmered to him while he was working. Who did something like that?

Thedric did. That was who.

He swallowed and wondered what Les would think if he shimmered away. He'd already disappeared on the man once, though, and it didn't feel right to do so again. So Thedric plastered a smile on his face and watched as his mate walked down the porch steps and came closer.

The house was clearly still under construction. The bare bones were there, but there was no porch railing, and someone was working on the roof. That wasn't where Les had come from, though. He'd been inside the house, which was a relief because Thedric could imagine how dangerous it was to work on a roof, and he didn't want Les anywhere close to that.

Would it be too much to demand his mate never do that again?

"Thedric?" Les asked as he stopped in front of Thedric.

Thedric stared. Miko had told him that Les owned his own construction company, which was why Thedric hadn't expected to find him dirty and looking like he'd been working. There was a smudge of dirt on Les's nose, and Thedric had to resist the urge to reach out and clean it off.

He cleared his throat and forced himself to look away. "I apologize for intruding on your day."

Les's lips stretched into a smile. "That's fine. I was about to take a break for lunch, anyway."

Thedric narrowed his eyes. His mate hadn't eaten lunch yet? It was almost two PM. Had he worked through lunch?

Les clearly needed someone to take care of him, and Thedric wanted to volunteer to do so. He doubted that would go down well, considering they didn't know each other, so he kept that instinct at bay and wondered how to tell Les they were mates.

"You should get some food," he said, trying to find a way out of the situation. He'd been the one to stick himself into it, and now, he had no idea how to get out.

"I probably should. Do you want to come with me?"

Thedric blinked. "You want to have lunch with me?"

"Well, I don't know if you've eaten or not, but I need food, and I'd rather talk to you without people spying on us."

Thedric looked around, but he couldn't see anyone but the people working on the roof. "Who's spying?"

Les indicated the house with his thumb. "I have no doubt that my nephew and his best friend are staring at us right this moment."

Thedric grinned when he looked behind Les and noticed two faces peeking from the window. "They are, or at least, I hope it's them."

Les laughed. "I have no doubt it is. Come on. There's a good diner not far from here."

He started walking, and Thedric quickly followed him. "I've already eaten."

"Then you can get a slice of pie or something. You clearly have a reason to be here, and I can't wait to find out what that reason is. I have to say that after the way you ran last night, I didn't expect to see you again."

"I apologize for that."

Les eyed him. "Are you going to explain?"

"I am. I promise."

Les nodded. "That's all I need. Take your time."

It was a relief to hear those words coming from Les, and Thedric obeyed. They both stayed silent as they continued walking, giving Thedric time to put his thoughts into an order that would make the situation slightly less disastrous.

He needed to tell Les they were mates. He had no idea how Les would react, but he might get up and leave. Thedric wouldn't follow if that was what happened. Not everyone wanted to be a mate to a supernatural creature, and while Les hadn't struck him as that kind of person, there was no way to be sure. However Les took it, Thedric wanted him to have a way to contact him so he could ask whatever question he was sure to have.

That was why as soon as they were in the diner and sitting at a booth, he took out a business card from his wallet and slid it over the table toward Les. "All the numbers and ways to contact me are on there," he explained. He always had a few business cards with his personal phone number on them, just in case, and today was already the third time he used one.

He'd given one to both Miko and Farley and had told them they could call him whenever they wanted.

He hoped they would.

Les appeared puzzled, but he took the business card and slid it into the small pocket of his flannel shirt. "Thank you. I'm almost afraid to ask what's going on."

Thedric opened his mouth, but a woman approached their table before he could say anything. She smiled at both of them expectantly, and Thedric found himself smiling back.

"Hello," she said. "What can I get you?"

Les went first, already knowing what he wanted, but Thedric wasn't sure. He'd already eaten, so maybe he could get just a cup of coffee.

Les's voice rumbled. "My friend here has already eaten lunch, but I thought he could get some pie. What do you recommend?"

"Cherry." The waitress didn't hesitate. "It's so good that you'll want to get an entire pie."

Les looked at Thedric in expectation, and Thedric nodded. "Cherry is fine. Can I also get some coffee?" He probably didn't need it, but it would make him feel better.

"Sure thing. I'll be right back with your food."

She left, and Thedric and Les were alone again. Thedric looked around, wondering if this was the best place to tell Les they were mates. Maybe he should have told him as soon as they saw each other today. There might have been a few people spying on them, but they'd been mostly alone and hadn't been in a public place. With no way of knowing how Les would react, Thedric was a little wary.

"You know you don't have to tell me anything you don't want to tell me, right?" Les said in a soft voice. "I mean, it's clear you're here to talk to me, but I can see how conflicted you are, and I want you to know that you can take your time. I have your phone number now, and I can give you mine so you can call me when you feel ready to do whatever this is."

It was tempting. Thedric had never been in this situation, and now that he was, he wished he weren't. He was happy he'd met his mate, but he hadn't expected all the awkwardness and how torn he'd be over everything.

But he and Les were both here, and there was no running away from what they were to each other. Thedric might as well tell Les he was his mate and see what happened.

He cleared his throat. "You're right. I'm here because I needed to see you and tell you something."

"I'm listening."

Thedric sucked in a breath. He couldn't look at Les while he said this, so he stared down at his hands. "I left your party so quickly yesterday because I didn't know what to make of the fact that you're my mate."

Les stared. He doubted anyone would have reacted differently. He couldn't believe the words that had come out of Thedric's mouth, yet at the same time, they felt right.

Of course he was Thedric's mate. That was why he'd been drawn to him since the first moment he'd seen him, why he couldn't stop thinking about him. It was why he'd been happy to see him just now and had invited him for lunch. There was a bond between them, and while Les couldn't feel it, it didn't make him any less Thedric's mate.

For a second, Les wondered if maybe Thedric was lying, but it didn't last more than that. Thedric didn't have a reason to lie to him. What would he gain from it? Not money, that was for sure. From the way he dressed and behaved, Les was pretty sure Thedric could buy himself anything he could ever want or need, and while Les was comfortable enough, he wasn't rich by any means.

"Les?" Thedric whispered.

Les cleared his throat. He didn't know what to say, but it was clear his silence made Thedric uncomfortable. It made sense. Thedric was probably afraid that Les would reject him, and he was getting anxious because Les hadn't reacted.

"Are you sure?" Les asked, even though he doubted there could be a mistake.

Thedric nodded. "I am."

"But look at how different we are. Wouldn't it make more sense for you to be bonded to someone else?"

"I didn't choose you. Fate chose you for me, and she doesn't make mistakes. You're my mate, and there's no denying that."

He'd know better than Les, so Les wasn't going to push. He didn't understand, though. When he thought of Thedric with someone, he imagined another Nix or maybe a shifter, but no one like him. Thedric needed someone who could stand by his side looking good in a suit. Instead, he'd gotten Les, who worked with his hands and spent his days getting dirty and sweaty.

Even though Les was Thedric's mate, it didn't mean they had to be together. Maybe Thedric was telling him this because he felt he should know, but that didn't mean they were going to be together.

Les's mind went back to his dream of having someone waiting for him at home. Now that he thought about it again, he couldn't stop imagining Thedric on his couch doing exactly that, and he liked that thought.

But first things first. He and Thedric had to talk things out, which was no doubt why Thedric was here.

"What now?" Les asked because he had no idea where to go from there.

Thedric looked disappointed, which told Les it wasn't the answer he'd expected. "I don't know. I wasn't sure how to react when I realized it, which is why I left so abruptly yesterday. I needed some time to wrap my mind around it, and I apologize for not telling you right away."

"Why did you? I'm human, so I wouldn't have known if you hadn't."

"Why *shouldn't* I tell you?"

Thedric said it as if it was the most natural thing in the world, and Les supposed it was for him. Supernatural creatures knew from the time they were born that there was someone out there for them and that if they were lucky, they'd meet that someone and be happy. Humans had no such things. There was talk of soul mates, but Les was already forty-four. He hadn't expected to meet his soulmate this late in his life.

Yet Thedric was sitting in front of him.

Les had no idea what to say, which was why he was grateful when the waitress stopped by their table and slid plates in front of them, but Les wasn't hungry anymore. Still, he picked up his knife and fork and cut a bit of his lasagna, then put it into his mouth and chewed. He could feel Thedric staring at him, and he knew he needed to give the man an answer, but he wasn't sure what to say.

"Thank you for telling me," he eventually went with.

"It's only natural that I did." Thedric was eating his pie, and every time he put a piece in his mouth, he made sounds that went straight to Les's cock. Would he sound like that in the bedroom? Les desperately wanted to find out, but he wasn't sure that was in the cards. He wasn't sure about anything at the moment.

He needed time.

So that was what he told Thedric.

"I need time."

Thedric froze. He avoided looking at Les again, put down his fork, and got to his feet. Les had no idea what was happening, but it wouldn't be the first time Thedric ran out on him, and he wouldn't stand for that. He might need time, but that didn't mean that waiting to talk about this would help either of them.

He put a hand on Thedric's wrist. Thedric stopped moving and looked down at him, but it was clear from his expression and how tense his body was that he'd run if he was given the opportunity.

"I never expected to be anyone's mate, let alone the mate of someone like you," Les explained. "It's going to take me a moment to wrap my mind around it. I really don't see how your Fate could have been so blind. We have nothing in common." Almost as if they didn't actually belong together.

Thedric sat down again, but he still looked confused. "I realize humans don't have mates, but surely, you can't deny that a lot of humans end up being mates to shifters and other supernatural creatures."

"I know that. I see enough of it in my family, and I'm not saying you made a mistake. I have no doubt that if you feel I'm your mate, I am. I just don't understand why me, and I've been alone for a long time. I'm not sure I know how to make a place for another person in my life."

"Not even a mate?"

"I'm not saying never. I'm not saying no or anything like that. I'm just asking for some time to wrap my mind around the fact that something I never expected to happen happened." And Les would probably want to talk to Niall and Val. After all, they'd been in his position not too long ago.

At least Thedric hadn't turned into a goat and fainted in a closet like Billy had with Niall.

Thedric slowly nodded. "I understand needing time and space. I won't push you into making any kind of decision. I just felt you needed to know, and I'm glad I told you. We both have things to think about and decisions to make. Many things will have to change if we decide to give our relationship a chance."

Les was glad Thedric understood but not surprised. They were mates, after all. "Exactly. There will be a lot of decisions we'll need to make, and honestly, it scares me. Thinking about all of this and knowing what I am to you is a bit overwhelming, that's all."

Thedric got up again, but Les didn't try to stop him this time. They stared at each other for a moment, and Les could see the yearning in Thedric's gaze. He felt similarly and wanted nothing more than to reach for Thedric and drag him closer, but it would be best for both of them to have some time to get their thoughts together. Besides, Les had Thedric's number now. He'd be able to call and text him whenever he wanted, to ask whatever question was on his mind, and hopefully, to get to know him without the pressure of having to go on dates.

"I hope to see you soon," Thedric murmured.

He was smiling this time, so Les knew he wasn't running. He was giving Les exactly what Les had asked for.

Time and space.

Chapter Four

Thedric had come to expect the many texts he got from Les every day. His day started with one and ended with another. They made him smile every time his phone vibrated, even though it was Les only some of those times. Mostly, Thedric's phone vibrated because of work, but he'd been going through life with a smile on his lips anyway.

And it was all thanks to Les.

Things were going well between them, especially considering what had happened when Thedric had told Les they were mates. He'd expected Les to take days, if not weeks, to think about it, but instead, Les had started texting him the same day. It had been a good night text, nothing more, but it had made Thedric smile, and every text he'd gotten from Les since then had done the same.

His phone vibrated on his desk, and he snatched it up to check who it was. When he saw it was Les again, he didn't waste time. It was a picture, and he cocked his head as he looked at it.

Which one? Les was asking.

Thedric didn't know anything about construction, but he was pretty sure this was a wall in the house Les and his people were working on. On the left was a pale green color, while on the right was a pale blue. Clearly, Les wasn't sure which color to choose, and while Thedric wasn't convinced he could really help when it came to these things, he was going to try.

Haven't the owners chosen? he sent back.

Les answered right away. *They told* me *to choose. I hate when they do that because it's not my house. They said it didn't matter to them, but I'm not sure which color to go with. You have good taste, so I thought asking you would be a good idea.*

I'm not sure about that. I don't know anything about construction or renovations.

You don't need to. I've seen how you dress, so I know *you have good taste. Now, tell me which one you'd rather have in your bathroom.*

Thedric stared at the picture for a moment. Knowing that people would live in a house where he'd chosen the colors, at the very least of the bathroom, made him feel strange. Still, there was only one answer he could give. *Blue.*

The three dots danced on his screen as Les wrote an answer. *Good choice. How's your day going?*

This was something Les often did. He sent Thedric pictures of whatever caught his eye, from the wall he had to paint to a picture of his coffee in the morning. Then, once they'd started talking, he'd ask about Thedric's day, his family, or whatever happened to be on his mind. Normally, Thedric would have found it ridiculous, but he kind of liked that Les was trying to make him part of his everyday life. They hadn't seen each other again, but somehow, it felt like Thedric had still gotten to know Les.

He knew that Les usually didn't eat breakfast. He wasn't hungry in the morning, and the thought of eating made him feel nauseous, so he just had coffee. Thedric, on the other hand, had been taught that breakfast was the most important meal of the day, so he tended to eat too much.

The two of them were different, yet they seemed to work together. Thedric was a bit worried things would change once they moved on from phone conversations to reality.

There were more than enough things he needed to worry about already. He suspected his parents knew something was happening, even though they had no idea what, and he'd been afraid one or both of them would barge into the office and make a scene. He hadn't contacted a divorce lawyer yet because he hadn't talked to Leiana, but considering how things were going, it was time.

I have important conversations coming up, so I should go, he texted Les.

Work?

Personal. I'll tell you when we see each other again, all right? Telling Les he was married wasn't something Thedric wanted to do on the phone, even though his marriage to Leiana had never been real. He'd need to explain all that to Les, and he'd need Les to listen to him. It would be too easy for Les to ignore a text conversation.

Does that mean you'll be taking me out on a date?

Thedric stared. Was that something he needed to do? He hadn't dated anyone in more than twenty years, and when he had before Leiana, everything had been orchestrated by his parents. They'd had to approve of the people Thedric dated, of the places where he took them, and of what they did. They hadn't been willing to risk Thedric getting someone pregnant, and they hadn't realized he much preferred dating males.

Do you want to go on a date? he sent back.

Yeah. Do you want me to organize it?

Please. I was thinking about it, and I honestly don't know what we could do.

Leave it to me, and good luck with your meetings.

Thedric stared at the screen for a moment longer after thanking Les, but Les didn't text anything else. He was at work, which meant he had things to do, and so did Thedric.

It wasn't something Thedric was looking forward to, so after sucking in a breath and telling himself everything would be all right, he got to his feet. He was in his suite of rooms in the house, which meant he'd have to trudge all the way to the other side to find Leiana. He'd been using that as an excuse to avoid the conversation, but if he and Les were going on a date, it meant things were getting serious.

They'd always been meant to become serious since Les was his mate. Maybe he should have told Leiana about Les right away, but he'd needed time, and he'd been afraid Les would end up telling him he didn't want to be his mate. Thedric had been terrified of rejection, and he still was, but Les was giving their relationship a real chance, even though he was doing it through texts and phone calls. He'd also asked Thedric out, which meant he wanted to see where things went.

With his heart in his throat, Thedric went looking for Leiana. He tried the library again when he walked past it, but the room was empty, as was the kitchen. The cook nodded when he peeked inside, and he left before she could ask if he needed anything to eat. He felt like if he tried, he might throw up, and that wasn't how he wanted to start this conversation with Leiana.

He found her in the garden. The weather was getting warm, and she'd always enjoyed working with plants and flowers. Thedric's parents thought it was beneath her and that she shouldn't get her hands dirty, but Thedric had always ignored them when they muttered about Leiana. They'd chosen her for him, and after twenty years, he didn't care whether or not they were happy about the result.

Leiana looked up when she heard Thedric walking closer. She smiled and took off her gloves, then got to her feet. She'd been crouched in front of an empty spot of earth, or at least, it had been empty before she'd started working on it. Thedric could see tiny plants poking from the ground now.

"I'm not used to seeing you in the garden," she said with a smile.

"And I'm not used to visiting it. We need to talk, though." If Thedric didn't go straight to the point, he was afraid he'd chicken out.

Leiana frowned. "That sounds serious. Is it your parents?"

Thedric looked around, found a bench under a tree, and

gestured toward it. "Maybe we could sit down."

Leiana was hesitant, but she nodded and followed him there. They sat, and even though they'd barely touched for the past twenty years, Thedric took her hand. "Do you remember back when we got married, we agreed to tell each other if we ever wanted a divorce?" he asked.

Leiana's eyes went wide. "You want a divorce?"

Dammit. This didn't feel like the right way to start this conversation, and Thedric was afraid he was messing everything up. "I've enjoyed being married to you. You're a friend, and you were the best person my parents could have chosen for me when it came to an arranged marriage. But I'm afraid I've met my mate."

Leiana's hand tightened around Thedric's. "You have?"

Thedric nodded and held his breath. They'd always said they'd be happy for the other if something like this ever happened, but now that it *had* happened, he wasn't sure how she'd take it. Either way, both their lives were about to change, something that hadn't happened to either of them in more than twenty years.

Thedric was terrified of the future and what it held, and he wouldn't be surprised if the same went for Leiana.

Les kept peeking at his phone, even when it didn't vibrate. He hadn't missed the amused glances Val and Niall kept shooting his way, but he didn't care.

He'd met his mate, and he wanted things between them to work.

It had taken him a moment to get used to the fact that someone out there had decided he and Thedric would be perfect together. He still wasn't sure that was true, and when he thought about it, he couldn't ignore how different they were and how many problems it could cause. He was afraid that eventually they'd have to deal with that, but for now, he was enjoying the first stages of their new relationship.

He and Thedric kept texting each other. Les usually initiated the conversation, but then, he'd been the one to ask Thedric for time and space. Thedric respected that and let Les take it at his own pace, and Les was grateful.

Even though he was starting to feel like maybe it was time to change things a bit.

That was why he'd teased Thedric about taking him on a date. He wanted to do that. He wanted to take Thedric out, to show him off to people, but before doing so, he might have to tell those people who Thedric was to him. He hadn't told anyone about the conversation he and Thedric had at the diner, and he wasn't sure how to bring it up with his friends and family.

Maybe it would be better not to, at least for the moment. He and Thedric could get through this first date and see how things went, and only then decide what the next steps would be. Thedric had mentioned having important private conversations to get through, and the same went for Les.

Since Thedric had told him to organize the date, Les decided to go ahead. He had no idea what Thedric was used to when it came to dates and going out, but he could imagine all too easily, and he doubted anything he could come up with would hold up to that. Thedric was used to luxury, and from the way he dressed, he was rich. That meant he could afford to do and buy whatever he wanted, while Les couldn't say the same. He wanted Thedric to experience his life and what he liked, so he decided to stick with something simple.

He booked a table at his favorite steakhouse, checked to see what movies were playing at the theater, and while there was nothing he wanted to watch, he kept that option open. Maybe after eating, they could take a walk? There was a nice park in town, and it was a usual place for couples to go. It wasn't anything special, but Les wasn't special. The sooner Thedric realized that, the better it would be for both of them.

Once he had everything ready, he texted Thedric again.

I organized our date for tonight. I hope that's all right?

It only took Thedric a moment to answer. *It's perfect. I want to see you as soon as possible.* The three dots continued dancing. *Does that make me sound too eager?*

Les laughed. He continued ignoring Val and Niall and decided to go sit on the porch steps to get a bit of privacy. He took his phone out and started typing his answer. *Even if it does, I'm just as eager. I can't wait to see you.*

Do we have to wait until tonight?

Les hesitated. He supposed that they didn't, but he was at work. Wasn't Thedric supposed to be doing the same? *What are you up to?* he texted back.

Only seconds later, Thedric appeared in front of him. Les rolled his eyes and put his phone away as he got to his feet. He'd barely gotten the chance to sit down, dammit.

But it was worth it to see Thedric.

The first time Les had met him, he'd thought Thedric was a bit stuck up, not just because of the way he'd been dressed during his birthday party. It was the way Thedric stood away from everyone, with his back straight and a cool expression on his face. He'd been perfectly dressed, and nothing on him had been out of place, from his hair to the way his tie hung around his neck.

He looked different today. Maybe it was because he wasn't in an uncomfortable setting in which he didn't know anyone, or maybe because of the meetings he'd mentioned. Whatever the reason, Thedric's cheeks were flushed and his eyes glittered. It seemed to be with happiness, but Les wasn't sure.

"What happened?" he asked as he reached Thedric.

Thedric almost vibrated. Les wanted to touch him and help him calm down, but he didn't know if there was anything he could do to make that happen.

"We need to be adults about this and have a serious conversation," Thedric said.

He was still smiling, which hopefully meant it wasn't bad. He was right, anyway. Les was forty-four and didn't want to play games, least of all with Thedric.

"I agree. I thought we could talk tonight during our date."

"Why don't we do it now? That way, we can go on our date and not have to think about any of this." Thedric looked up. "Unless you have to get back to work?"

Before Les could answer, Niall piped up from behind him. "We have everything under control," he yelled. "Take him away."

Les turned to glare at the house. Even though he couldn't see his nephew, Niall could clearly see him.

"We don't have to go now if you have something to do," Thedric said, his voice quieter.

Les wasn't about to miss this opportunity. "Why don't you shimmer us to my house? There, we can talk without anyone spying on us."

The smile bloomed back on Thedric's lips. "That sounds like a good idea."

Les held out his hand. Thedric stared at it for a second before taking it. Unlike Les's hands, which were blunt and rough, Thedric's hand was smooth, with long fingers. He had to be getting regular manicures, and Les wondered what Thedric thought of his significantly different hands.

He didn't have much time to wonder, because they appeared on his porch the next moment. He blinked, giving himself a few seconds to get used to the thought that he was home even though only seconds ago, he'd been at work. Hector seemed as startled as he was, because he was barking on the other side of the door.

Thedric looked wary, so Les quickly reassured him. "He's a great dog. I think we just startled him."

Thedric nodded, and Les was relieved he always carried his keys in his pocket. It meant they didn't have to go back to get his home keys. He unlocked the door, caught Hector before he could launch himself outside, and dragged him into the house.

It took a few moments to get everything settled. By the time he'd let Hector out in the backyard, he found Thedric sitting on his couch, looking uncomfortable. They might need to have this conversation, but it was clear there was something big on Thedric's mind and that he needed to get it out as soon as possible.

So Les sat next to him. "I don't know what you need to tell me, but whatever happened in your past is just that. I'm your mate, which I know is important to you, and I hope that whatever the issue is, we can work it out together."

Thedric sucked in a breath and nodded. "I hope the same, but you have to promise to listen to everything I have to say before you make decisions."

Les hoped he wouldn't regret it. "I promise."

Thedric stared at him for a moment before nodding. "All right. I'm not sure how close you are to my brother and how much you know about our family. My parents had arranged a marriage for him, but he'd met his mate, and he didn't go through with it."

Les barely knew Damick, but he knew who the man was. "I wasn't aware of any of that." He was slightly surprised that arranged marriages were still a thing, although he'd always known that many Nix were traditional. Clearly, Thedric's family belonged to that category.

"Damick got out of it. I suppose he had a good reason to do so, while I didn't."

Les stared. What was Thedric trying to tell him?

Thedric licked his lips and looked away. "I lost my brother back then. My parents told him never to come back, and he never did. I wasn't strong enough to stand up to them, just like I wasn't strong enough when they arranged a marriage for me the year before Damick's."

"You're married?" Les croaked.

Thedric looked at him. "I am."

Well, fuck.

"You promised to listen to everything I had to say before making decisions," Thedric quickly added.

It was clear Les didn't like what he'd just learned. Thedric wouldn't have in his place, either. *He* knew there'd never been anything between him and Leiana, but Les didn't. Les had no idea how these marriages worked, and Thedric would be the first to admit that his marriage to Leiana wasn't traditional the way his parents expected.

Les swallowed heavily. "You have kids?"

"No, and my marriage was never a real one."

Les stared at Thedric for a moment before nodding. "I'm listening."

Thedric was so relieved he had to take a moment to gather his thoughts. "It's how things had always been done in my family. My parents married because their parents decided they'd be a good match. They did the same for Damick and me, but I didn't have a reason to go against their wishes. I married Leiana, but that was all I was able to do, and the same went for her. We never shared a bed and realized early on that we never would. She was relieved that I didn't try to force myself on her, and I was relieved she didn't expect me to give her children or be a real husband to her. We've lived fairly separate lives since we got married, although we've become friends and live together."

She was Thedric's best friend and the one person who knew the real him. He hoped to change that soon and add Damick and Les to the list, but she was the only person on his side for now.

And he was about to divorce her.

"I don't know if I can date a married man," Les said slowly. "I understand everything you've said, but I can't do this."

Thedric smiled at him. "You promised to listen to everything I had to say, remember?"

"There's more?"

"Yes, but none of it is bad. Leiana and I agreed in the beginning of our marriage that if either of us ever met someone they wanted to have a life with, we'd get a divorce. We didn't do so back then because it was safer for her to be married to me. It meant her parents wouldn't organize another marriage for her, and it gave her a freedom she'd never had before. It's been twenty years, though, and considering how much money I made over the past two decades, I'll be able to help support her for the rest of our lives. She's never worked. It wouldn't have been proper, and while she does charity work and has many hobbies, it's one thing she was worried about. But our divorce will be amicable. We've already discussed things, and we both agree on what we want and don't want from it."

Les rubbed his face. "This is a lot to take in."

"I understand that, and I'm sorry for springing it all on you like this. I wasn't sure if there was another way to do so, and I thought it would be better to put everything out there."

"You were right. I wouldn't have been happy if I'd found out about this after we'd gotten together. I also understand why you and Leiana didn't divorce sooner. Your life is nothing like mine, but it makes sense for you to protect her from her parents and anyone else who would try to hurt her just because the two of you are getting divorced."

Thedric was relieved but still a bit worried. "Exactly. We've been married for so long that she's past the age at which her parents would be able to arrange another marriage for her. She'll be free to make her own decisions about everything in her life, including relationships. I want her to have that. She's been with me for twenty years, and she's supported me through all of it. It would have been easier for both of us to give in and have children, but we both refused to bring children into our situation, and I'm glad we didn't." Thedric hesitated, but he wanted everything to be out there. "That's not to say everything about the divorce will be easy."

"Are you still talking about you and your wife?"

"No, unfortunately. Leiana and I have already contacted divorce lawyers, and we know what we want. The problem will be our parents, especially mine. When Damick met his mate, they decided she wasn't up to their standards, and they kicked Damick out of their lives because he wouldn't leave her. They thought they still had the perfect son, but I was a disappointment to them because Leiana and I never had children. The divorce will make them angry, and they won't hesitate to let me know exactly how they feel. I'm afraid they might even attempt to intimidate you."

Les snorted and, to Thedric's relief, reached over to take his hand. "They can try, but as long as you want me, I'm not going anywhere."

"Are you sure? Because I know this is a lot. I should have stopped being a coward years ago and gotten divorced earlier. I was trying to protect Leiana, but a good part of the decision to stay married to her was also that it kept my parents off my back, at least over that. They still bothered me about children and everything else they think isn't right with me, but they couldn't force me to marry someone else. Leiana and I were lucky to be married to each other. I can only imagine what would have happened if my parents had chosen another woman."

Thedric had seen it happen often enough. He wasn't exactly friends with anyone, but he had acquaintances, most of them from work and from his time at boarding school and university. Most of the people he knew had entered arranged marriages like he had, and most of them were unhappy. Thedric couldn't say he'd been happy with Leiana, but he'd been content, which was more than he'd expected.

Les squeezed Thedric's hand. "I have to warn you that our relationship might not be easy. I'm old and set in my ways. I don't know if I can change my life to welcome someone as important as a mate."

That wasn't what Thedric had wanted to hear. "Are you willing to try?"

Thankfully, Les nodded right away. "I am. I understand how important mates are and how good our relationship could be if we manage to get over our differences."

"I think we will. We're mates, after all. In our case, I believe it's our differences that make us perfect for each other."

Thedric truly believed that. If his mate had been someone from his social circle, he doubted he'd have been as happy. He might even have been miserable. He didn't like that life, even though he had to live it. He'd been uncomfortable at the birthday party, but he'd also been able to relax more than he usually did during parties. There, he hadn't needed to keep up a mask so that no one would have something to criticize behind his back. He hadn't needed to make nice with some of the people present while avoiding others because his parents didn't like them. He'd been himself—tense, awkward, but himself. That was what being Les's mate meant to him. It meant leaving the person he'd been for his parents behind and finally allowing himself to find out what he truly wanted in life.

But maybe it was too soon to share all of this with Les. The man still appeared hesitant, which was entirely understandable. Thedric had dumped everything into Les's lap, but he realized Les would need time to wrap his mind around all of it, just like he'd needed time to wrap his mind around the fact that he had a mate. Now, though, everything was out in the open.

They could finally start their relationship on the right foot.

Les knew how lucky he was. As a human, he'd never expected to be someone's mate, but he'd seen enough of those relationships in his family to be aware of the fact that if he said yes to Thedric, they could both be blissfully happy for the rest of their lives.

Their very long lives, once they bonded.

Because Les would be bonded to Thedric, which meant his life would stretch out to match his mate's. It was something that freaked him out a bit, but at the same time, it also meant that he'd have most of his family by his side. He'd been thinking about how Flynn, Niall, and Val had bonded to shifters and would live long after he died, but that wouldn't be the case anymore.

It was all confusing, yet at the same time, it wasn't. There was only one choice, but he still had doubts. Thedric clearly didn't share Les's worry, though, and he was staring at him with an expectant expression. Les had already told him he was willing to give their relationship a chance, and he was, but he didn't want them to rush into anything, and he needed Thedric to understand that. As a Nix, Thedric was probably willing to bond right away and go from there, but Les would need more time.

"I'm not ready to bond," he finally said. He squeezed his hand to make sure Thedric understood it wasn't a rejection. "I didn't expect any of this to happen, and I still think we're too different. I think we should do this slowly, take our time to get to know each other, and see what happens."

Thedric nodded, but his smile had dimmed. "I

understand."

He probably did, but Les hadn't meant to push him away. "It doesn't mean we can't be together. I like the texts and calls, but I want to see you more."

Thedric's smile brightened again. "Well, I'm here. We have our date tonight, but unless you have to go back to work, we can spend the afternoon together, too. We can do whatever you want."

Those words gave Les wicked ideas. "Whatever I want?"

There had to be something in his tone that told Thedric what he was thinking about, because Thedric's cheeks flushed and he looked away. He looked pleased, though, so Les wasn't afraid that he'd offended him.

Thedric cleared his throat. "Yes, whatever you want. But I need to warn you that while I've been married, I haven't been unfaithful. I couldn't do that to Leiana, especially with the way our social circle would have talked about it behind her back. I respect her too much."

It didn't take a genius to understand what that meant. "So you haven't been with anyone for twenty years?" That even beat Les's dry spell. Thedric had to have a lot of control, and not just when it came to sex. Les enjoyed sex, but he also enjoyed the intimacy of being with someone, the casual touches and spending time together.

"I haven't, no. I remember how it works, but I doubt I'll last more than a few minutes if we start something. It's something you need to be aware of."

That wasn't a deterrent. If anything, it made Les want to get his hands on Thedric even more, and Thedric seemed to be on board with that. He was hesitant, but it was understandable, considering where they were in their relationship. Les was worried, too. He kept in shape through his job, but he didn't look the way he had when he was twenty or even thirty. His stomach wasn't flat, and he hadn't expected this to happen, so he hadn't manscaped. He doubted Thedric would care about any of that, but the feeling wasn't easy to ignore.

Les decided that the best way to get over the hesitancy they shared was to get started, so he pulled on Thedric's hand hard enough that Thedric moved toward him. Thedric's eyes went wide, but he didn't resist and landed in Les's lap. It took a bit of maneuvering, but eventually, working together, they managed to get Thedric on Les's thighs, facing him. Thedric's cheeks were redder now, and there was a shyness in his gaze that Les found adorable. It made him want to protect Thedric, even though Thedric didn't need to be protected. He was showing Les a side of himself that few people ever saw. Out there, Thedric was strong and in control. Here, with Les, he could allow himself to be vulnerable because Les would never willingly hurt him, and he knew it.

Les was humbled.

He cupped a hand over the back of Thedric's head, digging his fingers into Thedric's hair. He wanted to see it loose around Thedric's face, but now wasn't the moment. They both wanted something else, and Les was ready to give it to Thedric.

He pulled Thedric's face toward him. Once again, Thedric came without resisting, and their lips met. Les didn't surge forward like he wanted to, but instead, he took things slow, sliding his lips against Thedric's until he opened up to him. Once he had, Les dove in, skimming his tongue along Thedric's lower lip until Thedric caught it between his teeth.

Softness flew out the window as a fire ignited in Les. He tightened his hold on Thedric's head and held him close as he ravaged his mouth, taking what he wanted. Thedric was eager to give. His hands roamed Les's shoulders and chest as if he wanted to take Les's hoodie off, which would be perfect, but it would also mean that they had to stop kissing, and Les wasn't sure he was ready to do that.

He didn't know how long they kissed, but things got more urgent, as if he'd explode if he didn't get more. From the way Thedric clung to him, he was pretty sure he felt the same way, so maybe they could push this forward a little more.

Or a lot more.

Les tightened his abdominal muscles and pushed himself up. He almost fell backward, but Thedric helped him by turning around so it wasn't too hard for Les to deposit him on the couch without letting go of him. They stopped kissing for a second, and Les took advantage of that and pulled off his hoodie, dropping it beside the couch. His t-shirt had remained trapped in it, which meant his chest was bare. When he leaned forward, he caught Thedric staring at him. They froze for a moment, and Les had to resist the urge to cover himself.

But Thedric wasn't looking at him with disgust or annoyance. He was looking at him like he wanted him, and it was enough to give Les the courage to send his fears packing. He pushed up Thedric's soft sweater but didn't have the patience to take it and the shirt underneath it off. He hooked them both under Thedric's armpits, then lowered himself on top of him again.

He slotted perfectly between Thedric's legs as if he belonged there. He told himself not to read too much into it, but it was impossible not to, especially when Thedric kissed him again.

They both still wore their pants, but it clearly wouldn't stop them from getting farther into this. It would keep the mess to a minimum, and maybe next time, they could get naked and into Les's bed.

For now, this was perfect.

Thedric wrapped himself around Les as if he was planning on never letting go. Les was more than happy with that, and as they moved together, he thought that maybe this could work. Did it matter that they were so different? He wanted Thedric, and Thedric wanted him. Sex wasn't everything, and the fact that it was the best sex Les had ever experienced didn't mean the feeling would extend to the rest of their lives together, but the fact that their chemistry was off the chart helped soothe some of the fears he'd harbored.

Thedric wasn't playing with him. He wanted him and was willing to give him time, which was all Les needed.

Hopefully.

Thedric cried out, startling Les, who leaned back just in time to see Thedric press his head back against the couch pillow and screw his eyes shut. He shuddered in Les's arms, and Les knew what had happened. It spurred him into kissing Thedric again, and Thedric welcomed him, wrapping around him again and holding him tight as he moved. He chased his own pleasure, and with Thedric sated in his arms, it was easy to find it.

When Les came, it was with Thedric's name on his lips and his taste on his tongue. If this was what the rest of Les's life would be like, then maybe, it would be worth ignoring just how different the two of them were, just how out of place Thedric was on Les's couch, and focusing only on what they had in common.

Their bond.

CHAPTER FIVE

Thedric had always been great at avoiding his parents. It was a necessity when they were demanding and didn't listen to him, and it had become even more so after Damick had chosen his path and stepped away from the family. Their parents had poured all their expectations and demands on Thedric, and he'd needed to keep his sanity. He'd done that by avoiding them as much as he could. He was surprised word about the divorce hadn't gotten out yet, but he paid a lot of money so that his lawyer didn't go around telling people about his life, and it was good to see the man was worth it.

But it wasn't just the lawyer. Several servants worked at the house, mostly because Thedric's parents wouldn't have allowed him not to have servants, and he had no doubt they talked. Once it reached the ear of the people who worked for his parents, hell would descend upon him.

But keeping his distance had done wonders for his mood, although that might also be because of Les. Thedric wouldn't say their relationship was perfect, but it was as perfect as any relationship could be, as far as he was concerned. They were working things out, finding a way to be together, and giving each other a chance to make it work. That was all he'd wanted from Les, but he could see Les was still hesitant.

Yes, they were different. It wasn't only because Les was human while Thedric was a Nix. Their lives couldn't have been more different, but Thedric had to admit that was part of the appeal.

Even though he'd been born into wealth, it had never fit him. He hoped that being with Les would allow him to find his real self, and he was looking forward to it. He'd known that the first place his parents would visit in the attempt to find him was the house he shared with Leiana, which was why he'd avoided it as much as possible. He'd spent a lot of time at his office, and every evening, he went back to Les's house and spent the night there. He loved it and was glad Les welcomed him into his life and the home he'd lovingly renovated. Even though he and Thedric hadn't known each other back then, it still felt more like a home to Thedric than the house he shared with his wife ever had.

But he knew he needed to go back to the house and pack some of his things. He and Leiana kept in touch through emails and phone calls, and they'd met several times for the divorce proceedings. He was glad to see that the divorce hadn't changed anything between them. Leiana was still a lovely human being who wanted him to be happy, and it was making things go so smoothly that he hoped the divorce would be final soon. It would still take time, but the fact that he'd met his mate was making everything go even faster because of the laws the council had put in place.

Even though there was nothing Thedric wanted less, he left his office and shimmered back to the house he couldn't call home anymore. He scurried inside, just in case his parents were somewhere in the garden waiting for him—as ridiculous as that sounded. They hadn't even called, but he could feel a heavy cloud over his head, and he knew it wouldn't be long.

He closed the door behind himself and looked at the house. It had never felt like he belonged, and that hadn't changed. It was too big, too cold. He and Leiana could have changed everything, and they'd done so with the rooms where they spent most of their time, but they'd let it go when it came to the rest of the house. Their parents wouldn't have been happy to see them disrespect their gift, and besides, it wasn't like they spent a lot of time in the entrance or the formal living room.

"Thedric?" Leiana called from what seemed to be the library. That was the direction her voice came from, anyway.

Even though Thedric wanted nothing more than to run to his rooms and pack, he forced himself to go to the library first. He wasn't surprised to find Leiana curled up on one of the couches, a blanket covering her lap. She smiled when she saw him, and he found himself smiling back.

He wondered what would happen if he introduced Leiana to Les. He could understand why neither of them might want to meet the other, but they were both parts of his life, and he didn't think that would ever change. He was divorcing Leiana, but she'd always be his friend and the one person who had supported him for over twenty years.

"I was hoping it was you and not your parents," Leiana said.

Thedric grinned. "And I'm hoping they haven't found out about the divorce yet."

"Either that, or they know and are planning their attack."

That was a distinct possibility that Thedric didn't want to think about any longer. "I was wondering if you'd like to meet Les."

Leiana blinked. "I would love to, but I don't want to make things awkward for either of you."

"Wait here."

Thedric had never been impulsive, but the more distance he put between himself and his parents and his former life, the more he found himself acting without thinking too much. That was why he rushed out the door, headed back outside, and shimmered straight to Les.

Les happened to be home, and he jumped when he noticed Thedric next to him. He glared at him, but there was no heat behind it. "We're going to have to invest in those thingies that make it impossible for Nix to shimmer in and out of a place," he grumbled.

"I'll buy you as many as you want. I'd like you to meet Leiana." Thedric had to restrain himself from bouncing on his toes.

Les frowned. "Your wife?"

"Soon to be ex-wife, but yes. I realize it might be awkward for you, but she's an important part of my life, and I don't think that's ever going to change. She's my best friend, and you're my mate. It's important to me that the two of you get along."

Les looked down at himself. He was wearing jeans and a t-shirt under a flannel shirt. He was clean, but he still grimaced. "I'm guessing you want to do this now by how excited you are, but I'm not sure it's a good idea. I'm not dressed for it."

Thedric looped an arm around Les's waist and pulled him close. "You're perfect the way you are. I wish you'd believe me when I say it, and I hope you will in time."

Les peered at him for a moment, and when he eventually nodded, Thedric beamed at him.

Les shook his head, but there was a smile playing on his lips. "I guess we can go now. I know how complicated it is for you to find a moment to do this between my job and yours. I just hope it won't be a disaster."

"It can't be. The two of you are two of my favorite people in the world. Besides, Leiana understands that you're the person I need in my life. She's not angry at us and won't hold it against us."

Les sighed. "Let's go, then."

They did so after saying goodbye to Hector, who'd gotten used to having Thedric shimmering in and out of the house. He didn't bat an eye at it anymore and didn't get up from the couch as they left.

Les's eyes went wide when they got to the house, but Thedric ignored his shock and pushed the front door open. "Leiana!" he called out.

"Don't yell," Les scolded.

"Why not? It's my house, or at least it was. At the moment, it's Leiana's, but she's been thinking about selling it. It's ridiculous to have so much space when there are only one or two people living here." He tugged on Les's hand. "Come on. She was in the library and is excited to meet you."

Les didn't look as excited, but like everything in their relationship, Thedric hoped that it would be smooth going once it happened.

He wouldn't let it go any other way.

Les had already known how different his life was from Thedric's, but seeing the house in which Thedric had lived for the past twenty years reinforced that knowledge. How was Thedric supposed to leave this place to move into Les's small house?

They weren't at that stage yet, or that was what Les was telling himself. It was early for them to be moving in together officially, but Thedric had been spending most of his evenings and nights with Les. It might not be official, but he certainly didn't live here anymore, and Les wasn't sure he understood what was happening.

Why would Thedric not want to stay here? Seeing this place, Les expected Thedric to try to convince him to move here rather than the opposite, unless of course, Thedric wanted his wife to have the house in the divorce.

Thinking those words made Les's mouth taste bitter, but he told himself that Thedric had been honest with him and that his wife had never been anything more than a friend. He'd been hesitant to meet her, but he felt it was the right thing for him to get over his anger.

He wasn't angry at Thedric. Les wished Thedric had never gotten married since he didn't love his wife, but this wasn't his world, and he didn't fully understand it. He couldn't know how Thedric had felt twenty years ago, and even if he could, the circumstances now were entirely different. Thedric never hesitated to answer questions, and as far as Les could see, he was as honest as he could be. It would have been easy for him not to tell Les about his wife and get divorced, then act as if none of that had ever happened, but instead, he'd told him everything.

That had to mean something, right?

"This place is incredible," he murmured.

Thedric ignored him. He pulled Les up the stairs, and Les was almost afraid to touch anything. He wouldn't want to get anything dirty, even though he hadn't done much beyond painting today. The house he and the others were working on was almost finished, so it was just the last touches that needed to be completed.

But something about this place and Thedric made Les feel like a slumbering monster. He felt massive and like actively breathing might break something, which wasn't something he enjoyed. It also confused him. He had no doubt Thedric was happy to have met his mate, but how could he not want someone else? Les couldn't see a way for him to fit into Thedric's life when Thedric could have so much more. It felt like a bad idea for them to settle down together.

A beautiful blonde woman appeared at the top of the stairs. She wore a pair of black pants and a white blouse, and her feet were bare. Her blonde hair was loose around her face, and her smile made her even more beautiful—as if she needed it.

This was Thedric's wife? Thedric had told Les he'd always preferred men, so it wasn't a surprise that he hadn't been able to fall in love with his wife, no matter how beautiful she was, but still. Between the way she looked and the house, Les had never felt so much out of place.

"You never were so impulsive before," she teased Thedric as he and Les reached her.

Thedric gave her a wide smile. "I think it has to do with meeting Les." He pulled Les forward. "Les, this is Leiana, my soon-to-be ex-wife. Leiana, this is Les, my mate."

Les had no idea what to do. He felt like he was in a dream and like maybe Leiana was royalty. He was tempted to bow, but instead, he offered her his hand. He was pretty sure he was staring, which was rude, and he didn't want to make even more of a spectacle of himself.

Leiana placed her hand in his, and he carefully shook it. "It's a pleasure to meet you," he murmured.

"It truly is. When Thedric told me he'd met his mate, I was so happy for him."

Thedric had told Les, of course, but Les had a hard time believing it. How could Thedric's wife be happy that they were going to divorce because Thedric had met his mate? But Leiana truly seemed to be okay with all of this. Her smile was genuine, and her gaze warm.

The sudden sound of voices by the front door made Leiana and Thedric freeze. They stared at each other as the front door opened and people came in. Les turned to look at them, but Thedric sharply pulled him forward, startling him.

The three of them scurried down the hallway, but they didn't go far.

"What are they doing here?" Thedric asked.

"I don't know," Leiana whispered back. "They're your parents, not mine. They're your problem to deal with."

Thedric's expression told Les he wasn't looking forward to it, and considering what Les knew about Thedric's parents, he understood why.

"Do I really have to talk to them?"

A shrill woman's voice came from downstairs. "Thedric! Where are you?"

"You better go before they start poking around," Leiana said.

Thedric was pale, but he nodded. "Both of you stay away from them." He looked at Les, and for some reason, Les wanted to stop him. He could tell Thedric wished to avoid his parents, and if they were as toxic as he'd said, it would be best for him to go no-contact with them, but clearly, Thedric wasn't ready for that. That meant he'd have to explain himself, and apparently, the time to do so was now. His mother had sounded pissed, and Les had no doubt she'd find a way to get to Thedric even if he didn't go to talk to her now.

"Thedric!" she yelled again.

Thedric shared one last glance with Les before turning around and hurrying back to the stairs. Les and Leiana stared at each other for a moment, and Les wondered what he was supposed to do. Should he go home? How was he supposed to do that? Maybe Leiana could shimmer him back, but could she do so from inside the house? Thedric had mentioned that the only place where people could shimmer in and out was by the front door, and since he and his parents were in the entrance, it would be impossible for Les and Leiana to go there.

Which meant Les was stuck.

"I didn't hear you knock," he heard Thedric say.

He leaned sideways, wondering if he could get a peek at his mate. He could only see the top of Thedric's head from where he was, which was completely useless.

"What did you do?" Thedric's mother demanded to know.

"You're going to have to be more specific," Thedric told her.

Even though Les knew how nervous Thedric was about this conversation, he didn't sound like it. The mask he'd been wearing the first time he and Les had met was firmly back in place, and Les missed seeing the real man under it. Luckily, it wouldn't last for long.

"We heard a rumor," a man said, no doubt Thedric's father. "We were told that you and Leiana are getting divorced."

"Your father says that can't be true, but I trust the person who told me this," Thedric's mother interjected. "Now tell me the truth. Are you and Leiana getting a divorce?"

"We are," Thedric confirmed.

"Why? It's her, isn't it? I always knew she was a bad choice for you. She didn't even manage to give you children."

"She didn't give me children because we never shared a bed," Thedric snapped. "And the divorce isn't because of her. I initiated it. I told her I wanted out of our marriage."

"I don't believe that," Thedric's mother insisted.

"Well, you better believe it because I met my mate."

There was a moment of stunned silence, and Les was glad for it, but unfortunately, it didn't last nearly long enough.

"What are you talking about?" Thedric's father asked.

"Exactly what I said. Leiana and I never had a real marriage, and we agreed that if either of us met our mate, we'd get a divorce. I met my mate, so we're getting divorced."

"Who is she? Who are her parents?" Thedric's mother asked.

"He's human, and you don't know him, and I don't see how giving you details about him will change that."

"Human?" Thedric's mother asked at the same time that Thedric's father spat out the word, "He?"

Les swallowed. He'd known these two details about him would be a sticking point. As a male, he couldn't give Thedric children. As a human, he wasn't part of Thedric's world. It didn't matter that Thedric's parents didn't sound like they loved or even cared about Thedric. They were right about these things.

Les didn't have much to give Thedric, and listening to him tell his parents about him reminded him of that.

"Yes, he's human," Thedric confirmed. In any other circumstance, he'd have been amused by the shock in his parents' expressions. As it was, he knew they wouldn't leave unless he kicked them out, and he had every intention of doing exactly that. First, he'd put everything out there so they knew what they were going up against.

"That can't be possible. You can't allow this to happen," Thedric's mother said.

Her eyes blazed, and Thedric had no doubt that if she could, she'd have already dragged him out the door to find him another wife. She'd been angry with Leiana the past few years because Leiana hadn't given Thedric children, and she'd been convinced it was Leiana's fault, but now, she knew the truth. That wouldn't stop her from trying to find a new wife for Thedric, unfortunately.

"I'm not *allowing* anything to happen. I was happy to meet my mate, and he and I are together. That's why Leiana and I are getting a divorce. There was never any kind of romantic love between us, and there never will be."

Thedric's mother snorted. "Romantic love? Who said anything about romantic love? That's not why we chose her for you. We chose her because of who she was, her ability to give you children, and what she'd bring to the family. Your mate cannot bring anything to the table."

She said the word *mate* with so much scorn that it shocked Thedric, but he should have expected it. He *had* expected it. He only had to look at Damick's situation. His mate was a woman, and she'd given him a child. Their parents should have been happy, but instead, they'd kicked Damick out because his mate couldn't bring anything to the family. Unless it was someone they approved of, they'd do the same to Thedric's mate, and who and what they were would never matter.

"Think about it," Thedric's father said, sounding reasonable. "This person cannot give you children. I don't know who he is, but he's a human, which means he's not part of our world. What can he give you?"

"Love. Happiness. He's been giving me that since we met."

"None of these things matter."

"They do to me, and I won't change my mind. Leiana and I are going through with the divorce, and my mate will hopefully agree to bond with me. And if you try anything to stop that from happening, I'll make sure to report you to the council."

Thedric's mother hissed. "You wouldn't dare."

"Wouldn't I? I'll never be able to do anything that makes you happy. Every time I try, you have more demands, and they never stop coming. I'm done trying to make you happy. I'm done trying to make anyone but myself and my mate happy. You're going to have to wrap your mind around that and deal with it, because it's not going to change."

The sound of footsteps made the three of them look up. Thedric had told Les to stay back, but instead, he was rushing down the stairs. He seemed intent on walking past Thedric and his parents without even looking at them, but Thedric's father placed himself in Les's path. Les peered at him, looking as if he was wondering what would happen if he tried to push him aside.

Thedric cleared his throat. He didn't want things to turn violent, and no matter how nasty his father was, he'd never raised a hand to anyone. Luckily, the sound Thedric made was enough to break the moment, but the tension was still there, so thick it was almost hard to breathe.

"This is my mate, Les," he introduced.

Both his parents looked at Les like he was an insect that needed to be stomped on. Thedric reached for Les, and pain flashed through his chest when Les tilted his body away from him. He didn't want Thedric to touch him.

Thedric's mother dismissed Les and turned her attention back to Thedric. "We won't allow you to do this."

Les took the opportunity to slide past them and open the front door. Thedric moved to stop him from leaving, but his father grabbed his shoulder and kept him in place. Thedric turned around, glaring at him, but by the time he'd shaken his father's hand off, the front door had closed.

"You don't have to *allow* me to do anything," Thedric snapped. He wanted to go after his mate but needed this conversation to be over first. If they attempted to put themselves between him and his mate, he wouldn't hesitate to report them to the council. That threat wasn't empty, even though they didn't realize it yet.

He squared his shoulders. "I'm an adult, and no matter how hard you try, you won't be able to get anyone to declare me incapable of taking care of myself like you attempted with Miko. I've been taking care of myself and Leiana for twenty years, and I don't need you. I'm done trying to get your approval. You'll never give it to me, and it doesn't matter anymore. I finally have everything I've ever wanted in life."

"You already had that before," his mother protested. "I know you think he's your mate, but you have to see that's just not possible."

"The only thing I see is that I'm in love with him."

"A divorce would be a scandal. What will everyone think?"

"I don't care."

Now that Thedric was away from his parents' influence, he'd never have to deal with their social circle again. He didn't have to care what they thought of him and his actions. He only cared about what Les and his family thought, but he doubted his parents could understand that. They'd only ever cared about how they looked and how people viewed them. Feelings, friendship, and family had never mattered to them, and that would never change. Thedric was done trying to make them proud and get them to love him.

"If you can't accept the divorce and my bonding to Les, then you need to leave us alone. I don't want to see you again until you can accept that." Which he doubted would ever happen. "And don't think of coming here. I'm moving out, so you won't find me in this house. We'll also make sure to change the locks and put up stronger shields to keep you out."

Thedric's mother scoffed, but if she wanted to play, she'd soon find out that Thedric wouldn't hesitate to stand up to her. He was done bowing to her and her demands.

He was free, and it was thanks to meeting his mate.

But Les had left, probably because he'd heard the nasty things Thedric's parents had said about him. Thedric wanted to reassure him, but he also didn't want to leave Leiana alone with his parents. He was angry. His parents had sent Les running, and he hated them for that.

"Leave," he ordered.

"You can't force us," his mother retorted.

"I can call the enforcers. I can have a team here to drag you out in minutes." That probably wasn't true, but she didn't need to know that.

She looked like she was about to fight back, but thankfully, Thedric's father put a hand on her shoulder. "We should go," he said.

"How can you say that? He's ruining his life and ours."

"Give him time to think. I'm sure he'll realize we're right soon enough."

Thedric snorted. He didn't have to tell his father there was a fat chance of that happening. He suspected his father knew and was just trying to appease his wife and avoid having

Thedric call the enforcers.

Thedric stared them down as they finally realized there was nothing they could say to make him change his mind. His mother no doubt wanted to continue pushing, but she eventually allowed Thedric's father to pull her away.

Thedric watched them as they left the house. The door closed behind them, and he finally allowed himself to relax. His shoulders slumped, and he leaned a hand against the door, needing the support to stay on his feet.

He'd done it. He'd told his parents everything, he'd stood up to them, and he'd won.

"I tried to stop him from leaving," Leiana said from the top of the stairs.

Thedric sighed. "Don't worry about it. It couldn't have been easy for him to hear all of that."

She nodded. "Will you go after him?"

"Always."

Les stared at his front door. He'd run from Thedric, his palace of a house, his wife, and his parents. He'd used Thedric's app to do so.

And now, he was standing in front of his house, wondering what he was supposed to do.

Over the past couple of weeks, he'd gotten used to having Thedric around. He'd settled into this new life with someone by his side, and it had felt so natural. Now, he knew it wasn't. Nothing about his boring, old life would be natural for Thedric, and even though Thedric might not see that at the moment, Les could.

Thedric was blinded by the fact that they were mates. He wouldn't listen to anyone telling him it wasn't a good idea, including Les. Les hadn't tried hard to push him away because he'd wanted everything Thedric was offering. He still did, but now, he understood how selfish it made him.

Thedric deserved so much better. He could *have* so much better.

With a huff, Les unlocked his door and went inside. His truck was still at the house where he'd been working earlier, but he could get a Nix to shimmer him there later and pick it up. Right now, he wanted nothing more than to hide, and the only place where he felt safe to do so was his house, even though it was the first place Thedric would look for him.

That was why he wasn't surprised when a knock came on his door about fifteen minutes later. Hector was sniffing around the backyard, but Les was tempted to call him inside and use him as a shield. Hector would never hurt anyone, least of all Thedric, but he'd be a distraction and Les felt he needed one.

What was he supposed to tell Thedric? The truth would probably be a good start, but he wasn't sure what the truth was.

"Les?" Thedric called through the door. "I know you're here. You don't have any reason to hide from me. My parents are gone, and they're not coming back."

Les was quiet as he walked to the front door. He wanted nothing more than to open, but he was also terrified of doing so. He needed to do the right thing, but what was it?

He pressed his forehead against the door and closed his eyes. Thedric, the other half of his soul, the mate he'd never expected to have, was here to talk to him. Les owed him the conversation, even though it was the last thing he wanted to do. He didn't want to lose Thedric and the life they were building together, but could he really hold Thedric back?

"Les?" Thedric called again.

Les sucked in a breath and opened the door. Thedric was as beautiful as always, maybe even more so. There was a fire in his gaze, and his cheeks were flushed. He looked like he'd gone through a fight and had come out the winner, which was probably what happened.

Thedric smiled. "There you are. I was worried I was talking to an empty house."

Les shook his head and stepped out, closing the door behind himself. The gesture made Thedric frown, but he didn't call Les out on it.

Instead, he said, "I talked to my parents. I told them that you're my mate and that Leiana and I are getting divorced. They know there's nothing they can do to separate us."

But they'd already done enough. The words felt stuck in Les's throat, but he forced himself to say them. "Your parents are right."

For a moment, Thedric looked like he didn't understand what Les was talking about. Then, his expression turned horrified. "What are you talking about? My parents have never been right about a thing in their life."

"Look at this place. I've just seen the place where you've lived for the past twenty years now, and it can't compare. You're used to luxury and having everything you want, and I can't give you that."

The fire had never left Thedric's gaze. It flared hotter now, probably stoked by anger. "So you think my parents are right?"

Les shrugged. "I don't know. We've always known we were different, but I thought we could make it work anyway. I'm not sure about that anymore."

"Just because of what they said? Les, these are people who believe I should force Leiana to carry my children. Why would you believe anything they say?"

Les was horrified but didn't have an answer to give Thedric. He didn't know why he believed Thedric's parents more than he believed Thedric. He'd told himself it was because they'd raised Thedric and would know what he deserved and needed better than anyone else, but that wasn't the truth, was it?

Les rubbed his face with both his hands. "I don't know anything anymore."

"I know how my parents are. They get under your skin, then twist everything until you believe whatever they say. They've done it to me repeatedly, so much so that I stayed after what they did to my brother. Even then, it wasn't enough for them. I'm not planning on trying to keep them happy anymore, and you shouldn't, either."

"But I can't take you away from all of that, from your world." And it was so far from Les's world that Les wondered if there was a way to mesh them together.

"What my parents have always wanted more than anything is control. Control over my brother, over me, and over everything in our lives. When we were children, it was easy because we had to follow their orders. We didn't know any better. Hell, I didn't know any better until recently. I allowed them to take my brother from me, but I won't allow them to take my mate. I'm finally strong enough to stand up to them. Damick is back in my life, but I've missed so much. They ruin everything they touch and are trying to ruin our relationship, too."

"But I'm not rich. I can't give you kids. I'm not even sure I *want* kids, for fuck's sake. The two of us being together doesn't make sense, and I don't understand how you don't see it."

"Since the very first day, I've been convinced that our differences are our strengths. I believe they're the reason we fit so well together. I know you don't feel the same, but I hope that in time, you'll realize I'm right." Thedric hesitated. "Whatever happens between us, Leiana and I are going through with the divorce. We should have done it long ago, and I don't want to waste one more second. But I'm struggling to understand what you're saying. Are you trying to break up with me?"

Les wasn't sure there was a way to break up with your mate. He supposed he could just walk away, and even though he'd be uncomfortable, he wouldn't be the one hurting. No, that would be Thedric. Even though they hadn't bonded, he felt the bond between them strongly, and he'd feel its loss just as strongly. Was that something Les could do to him? Was it something Les *wanted*?

If Les allowed himself to be selfish and honest, he could admit that he wanted things to go back to how they'd been before this mess. He liked having Thedric in his home and his bed, to come home to him at night, and to spend the evening on the couch making out and watching bad TV. He didn't know if he could give that up, especially when Thedric was so convinced of what he wanted.

"Can you give me a little time?" he asked, hoping Thedric could do so again. "I'll understand if you can't, but I have to sort out my thoughts. I don't want to believe your parents are right, but I can't avoid wondering if they are."

"And taking some time to think things over will help you?"

"I hope so." That was the only answer Les could give Thedric.

Thedric nodded. "I'm not going anywhere. Take as much time as you need, and I'll be waiting for you when you're done. I'm not going to take my things away from your house. It's my home now, too, and I won't let you kick me out permanently. I'll stay away for now, but not forever."

The words made Les smile. Maybe things weren't as dire as he thought after all.

Chapter Six

Thedric had been afraid many times in his life. He'd been scared of not being up to the standards his parents had set up for him. He'd been scared of losing them and his brother. He'd been scared he wouldn't be able to deal with being married to Leiana.

But he'd never been as terrified as he was now.

Was he going to lose Les? He didn't want to contemplate that possibility, but he and Les hadn't talked in several days, and it was taking everything Thedric had not to contact his mate. Les had requested more time to think things through, and Thedric wanted to honor that request, even though it felt like it had torn his heart out. None of the fears he'd felt before ever came close to making him feel so lost. He didn't know what he'd do if Les decided this was too much for him. When they'd met, his life had taken a turn he'd never expected it to take, and he couldn't go back. He didn't *want* to go back, which in the end, was what mattered.

For twenty years, he'd been unhappy, and it had hurt, but he'd never done anything about it. Meeting Les had allowed him to break through the barriers he'd put between himself and the life he wanted, but losing him wouldn't put them back up. He was done going along with what his parents wanted. He was done going along with what their society and social circle thought and believed. He was free and didn't think he'd have had the strength to make that happen if it weren't for Les, even though he'd started the process when he'd decided to reach out to his brother.

Maybe Thedric would have to make that enough. He had his brother back, along with the rest of Damick's family. Miko and Farley were always texting Thedric, sending him funny pictures and cat videos. It was as if Thedric had always been part of their lives, and he didn't want that to change.

He wouldn't *allow* it to change.

A knock on the door made him turn his head toward it. He didn't get up from the small bed he was lying on, though, and he didn't tell whoever was at the door to come in. It could only be a handful of people, and either they'd leave or come in without waiting for an answer. He'd moved in with his brother and his family after the fight with Les, and they didn't consider privacy important.

The door opened.

Miko peeked in, met Thedric's gaze, and rolled his eyes. "You could have said something."

"Would it have stopped you if I'd told you I didn't want to talk to you?"

"Of course not, but at least I would have known you were alive before I opened the door."

"Well, I'm alive. You can go now that you made sure of that."

Instead of going, Miko closed the door and came to stand next to the bed.

When Thedric moved in, he hadn't known what to expect. He'd just known he couldn't stay in the big house with Leiana, and he didn't have anywhere else to go. He'd called Damick, and as soon as Damick heard his voice, he'd known something had happened. When they'd met, he'd pulled Thedric into his arms, and Thedric had allowed himself to break down. Apart from Les, Damick was the only person with whom Thedric felt comfortable enough to be that vulnerable, and it felt like it had fixed their relationship just a bit more.

They were putting things back together, and while it would take time to be comfortable with each other again, at least they'd taken the first steps. With Thedric free of their parents, it was easier, and when Damick had told Thedric he could move in with him and his family, Thedric had said yes. He wanted more time to get to know them and didn't want to return to the house where he'd lived for so long.

So here he was, stretched out on a small bed, staring at a white ceiling and being judged by his nineteen-year-old nephew.

Miko sighed and sat on the edge of the mattress. "He just asked you to give him time. He didn't tell you he didn't want you."

Thedric swallowed. Miko and Farley had both been trying to make him feel better, but he wasn't sure anything could make that happen. "I know."

"Yet you're acting like he kicked your ass out and told you never to come back."

Because that was what it felt like. "What are the odds he'll be able to get over what my parents said? He was always a bit resistant and kept saying that he couldn't offer me much and that our lives were too different, but I dismissed those fears, and I shouldn't have. Maybe if I'd listened to him, I wouldn't be here now. Maybe he wouldn't have kicked me out of his life."

"He didn't."

The door opened again, and Thedric wasn't surprised to see Farley walk in. He carried a tray with three mugs on it and slid it onto the nightstand before closing the door and sitting on the floor, facing Thedric. He grabbed one of the mugs, then stared at Thedric until he sat up and did the same.

Thedric took a sip, smiling at the taste of hot chocolate. His parents would have wrinkled their noses because it was such a common beverage, but Thedric loved it, even though the weather was getting too warm to drink it.

"Thank you," he whispered.

Farley nodded. "You're welcome. Now, are you ready to stop moping around?"

"I've been taking time for myself. My life has changed significantly over the past few weeks, and I'm still reeling from it. That's not moping." Actually, he was, but Thedric would never admit it.

Farley could clearly read him because he narrowed his eyes. "That's bullshit."

"He's definitely been moping," Miko confirmed.

"Why are you ganging up on me? I lost my mate. Shouldn't you be nice?"

"You didn't lose him. You're giving him time, which was what he wanted and maybe what the two of you need. You went from living with your wife to living with Les, and I have no doubt it's what you wanted, but have you thought about how the rest of your life has changed? Are you going to live here forever? Or until Les takes you back? What will you do if he doesn't? And what will you do if he does? How will your two lives mesh together?"

Farley nodded. "You need to start planning your future."

Thedric felt like he didn't have one, but these two weren't wrong. His life had changed so much in so little time that it made his head spin, but he couldn't spend the rest of his life on this bed.

He took another sip of hot chocolate to give himself time to think. "I suppose I could at least look at houses," he said slowly. He'd been avoiding it because he hoped Les would take him back and that he could move in with him again, but what would happen if Les needed more time or if he decided all of this was too much for him?

Farley seemed to approve. "You don't have to buy a house. You can just look at places where you'd like to live. Maybe think about what you want from your future home, you know? That mansion where you used to live is nothing like you."

Miko and Farley had come around to help Thedric pack some of his things when he'd moved in with Damick, so they'd seen the place. Unlike most people who visited, they hadn't been in awe. Farley had wrinkled his nose and mentioned how big the place was, and Miko had asked how much the upkeep cost. Thedric couldn't answer because he wasn't the one who took care of his accounts, which he now realized could be a problem. He'd always wanted his life to change, and now, it had. Whatever he made of those changes and the opportunities they brought was up to him. He could continue moping and staring at the ceiling, or he could finally take his life in hand and make it what he'd always wanted.

The decision was his, and it was time for him to make it.

Les wasn't feeling great. It wasn't physical, which he'd have been able to ignore like he always did. No, he wasn't feeling great because he was an asshole and had no idea how to fix it.

He'd pushed Thedric away again. Instead of trying to fix things with him, Les had asked for more time, but he hadn't realized that wasn't what he needed. No, what he needed was for him and Thedric to talk things out so he could finally accept that Thedric could make his own decisions. Instead, he'd acted as if he was forcing Thedric to be with him, which definitely wasn't the case.

And now, here he was, moping around his house, all alone.

He leaned back against the couch and stared at the ceiling as he scratched Hector's head. Nothing had changed between him and Thedric, or rather, nothing about their situation had changed. They were still mates, and they were still extremely different. Even if Thedric was able to get past all of that, Les would still feel like he was taking way too much from his mate, and that wasn't fair. So where did this leave him?

Sitting on his couch and staring at the ceiling.

A knock on his door made him frown because he wasn't expecting anyone. It also made him wary. He doubted it would be Thedric, who would have been welcome, even though Les still had no idea what he was doing. He'd asked Thedric for time, and Thedric would give him that, which meant he wouldn't be visiting him until Les reached out to him.

But he wasn't the only one who visited Les. Les had an entire family who had made a habit of sticking their noses into his life, and he wouldn't be surprised if one of them had somehow found out what had happened with Thedric.

Les grimaced. Actually, he'd be surprised if no one knew. Thedric wasn't close to his parents, but he had his brother and his nephew, and Les knew Miko. He was also part of Les's family, even though they didn't know each other well. Surely, if he knew what was happening, he'd want to support his uncle.

Which meant he might be the one knocking on Les's door.

There was another knock, and Les sighed. Whoever it was, they wouldn't just leave, and he didn't want to have to listen to them continue knocking. He dislodged Hector's head from his thigh and got to his feet as a third knock came.

"I'm coming, I'm coming," he grumbled as he moved, sounding like his grandfather. When had he become so old?

He could see several people on the porch from the living room window, and while he wasn't looking forward to finding out what kind of intervention they were planning, he doubted he'd have a choice. One of them would probably find a way into the house if he didn't answer, and his safe place would be invaded.

He might as well find out what was happening.

He opened the door and stared. This *definitely* was an intervention, and they wouldn't take no for an answer. Niall was the one who'd knocked, and he had his hand raised as if he'd been ready to continue doing so until Les opened. Behind him was Billy, his mate, along with Flynn, Jude, and even Val and Simon. Simon looked a bit uncomfortable, no doubt because he didn't know Les as well as the others, but he was family, too.

Les sighed. "I'm almost afraid to ask what you're doing here."

Niall pushed past him to walk into the house. He looked around as if he thought Les was hiding someone, and Les stared, wondering if he had it in himself to ask. Did he want to know what was going on in Niall's mind?

"I thought the house would be in worse shape," Niall said.

"Why would it be?"

"Aren't you moping? You fucked up, and now you don't know how to fix things."

Les gestured at the others to come in. "You don't know what you're talking about," he said as he headed back toward the living room.

Hector was still on the couch, looking wary at the number of people in Les's home. He recognized them, though, and his tail thumped a few times.

Les flopped back onto the couch next to the dog and started petting him again. That was good enough for Hector, who snuggled against Les, clearly happy to let him deal with the invaders.

Niall followed Les into the living room because of course he did. "We know what's going on," he declared. "You were an idiot, and now you're moping."

"What do you want?" Even if he did know what Les had done, Les doubted he could help. No matter how much he wanted Thedric in his life, the differences between them would never vanish, and no one could do anything about it.

Niall sat on the coffee table and stared at Les. His expression changed from humor to seriousness in a way Les hadn't expected from his nephew. Niall wasn't usually like this, which meant he knew what he was talking about. Thedric had probably talked to his nephew, who had then talked to Niall's family.

And now, here they were.

"Sorry, we're late," a voice said from the entrance.

Les closed his eyes. He wasn't even surprised to recognize Miko's voice.

"What is he doing here?" he asked no one in particular.

Flynn sat next to him on the couch and patted his knee. "We thought he'd be in the best placed to talk to you about his uncle. He understands the problems you're facing better than any of us."

Les wasn't sure about that. Miko and Thedric hadn't known each other long, even though they were related.

But it looked like he wasn't getting out of this.

Miko and Farley walked into the living room, attached at the hip like always. They looked around, and while Farley stayed back, Miko made a beeline for Les. He stood in front of him, glaring down at him, and Les felt like he deserved it.

"You're making my uncle miserable," Miko accused.

Les stared. "You know everything?"

"I think so. I talked to him, and he explained that you feel the two of you are too different and that he would be giving up too much to be with you."

That was the heart of it, so Les nodded.

Miko sighed. "But don't you see? He's already made his decision. He wants you, and that's not going to change, even if you push him away. The only thing *that* will achieve is to make both of you miserable."

"It doesn't change how different we are. I saw his house.

How can this place compare?"

"It doesn't have to compare. You know how miserable my uncle was for all those years. Living in a massive house didn't change that, but you can. You're not taking anything away from him by being his mate. If anything, you're giving him something he never thought he'd have. I understand why it seems like a lot and why you're hesitant, but shouldn't you at least give him a chance to show you how much he wants this? Why are you pushing him away when you're each other's future?"

"I understand how all of this feels," Flynn interjected. "I was hesitant, too, but I'm glad I gave my bond a chance. As confusing and scary as it is, having a mate is wonderful. It's a relationship like nothing you've ever had, and even though it might seem like Thedric is giving up a lot, he really isn't. What you'll be able to give back is something he isn't willing to give up, and you shouldn't, either. Besides, have you thought that maybe he *wants* to give all his old life up?"

"You haven't seen his house." And he hadn't heard Thedric's parents, but Les had, which made this even more ridiculous. No one would hesitate to leave them behind, so why was Les doubting Thedric?

"I don't have to have seen it to know it's not as important as you. The house is just that. A house. You're his mate, and just like with any other supernatural creature, that's what matters to him. I'm sure he can buy a dozen houses if he wants, but he only has one mate, and that's you."

And Les had pushed Thedric away. He still didn't understand how anyone could choose him over everything Thedric would be leaving behind, but he was starting to realize that he didn't *have* to understand. Thedric had been at ease in this house. He'd clearly felt at home, which was what Les had wanted. When they'd been at the mansion, though, Thedric had been uncomfortable. He'd been excited to introduce Les to his ex-wife and to pack his things to move them here, but he still hadn't been like himself. That place had been too big, not comfortable enough. It was cold and didn't look anything like the idea Les had made himself of the place Thedric should call home.

But his house was. *Les* was.

Since Thedric was done moping around, he'd decided he needed to go to the office. He'd hoped it would help distract him while he attempted to find a way to convince Les he wouldn't regret anything when it came to choosing him for the rest of his life, but he was finding it hard to work. He was obsessed with going back to Les, which made sense, considering everything. He wanted to beg Les to give him another chance, but he'd told Les he'd give him space and time, and he wanted to honor that request like he had the first time Les had requested it. It wouldn't help either of them if he pushed and broke something, so even though it was the hardest thing he'd ever done, he stayed right where he was.

But there was no work happening.

He was relieved when someone knocked and wondered what they'd think if he kissed them to thank them. When the door opened and Miko peeked in, he knew his nephew would probably be happy. He and Miko were getting along, and while Thedric had never been overly affectionate with anyone because it just wasn't done in his world, Miko hadn't been raised that way. Since Thedric had moved in with his brother's family, Thedric had seen them hug several times. He'd seen Miko cuddle with his mother and kiss his father's cheek, even though he was an adult. It was good to see, and it warmed Thedric's heart to know that the next generation wouldn't be as cold as he and his brother had been expected to be.

"What brings you here?" he asked as he gestured at Miko to come in. As expected, Farley was right behind him and closed the door.

"Maybe I missed my favorite uncle," Miko teased.

"I might believe that if I didn't know you don't have other uncles. Besides, we saw each other a few hours ago. Surely you didn't have the time to miss me."

The way Miko grinned told Thedric he was hiding something. That was often the case, and while Thedric wanted to ask, it probably was none of his business. If Miko wanted to tell him what was happening, he would.

But Thedric was slightly afraid to find out.

Miko and Farley stopped in front of the desk. They looked at each other, then back at Thedric. "We're here to tell you that you need to get your head out of your ass and get Les back," Miko declared.

Thedric blinked. No one could say his nephew wasn't blunt. "It's what I want, but he's not comfortable having me around for now. He asked for time to think."

"And it's great that you were willing to give him that since he needed it, but he's had enough of it." Miko sat on the edge of the desk, twisting so he could look at Thedric. "I know you want to give him everything he needs, but you also have to think of yourself. It won't be good if you focus only on Les's needs and ignore yours. Don't think about him for a moment. What do *you* want right now? What do you need to be happy?"

Thedric closed his eyes and thought. It didn't take long. "I want to see Les. I want to find out what's going on, why he's so hesitant, and to soothe his fears. I want him to bond with me and to be happy."

He opened his eyes to find Miko and Farley both smiling at him.

"Then do that," Farley said, grinning. "It's time to show

him what you want and what you can give him."

"But why if he hasn't gotten over his fears?"

"Then help him get over them. Being alone in his house moping around isn't going to help him."

Thedric narrowed his eyes. "How do you know he's alone in his house moping?"

"We might have taken part in a small intervention his family organized," Miko explained, sounding unrepentant. "We didn't say much, but we were there and heard what he said."

Thedric shouldn't be surprised. "So you know he believes we're too different."

"We do, and I can even understand why he feels that way, but I know you. You don't want that mansion. You don't want the life your parents want for you. You'll be happier with Les in his small house than you've ever been with your wife in that mansion."

"I already told him that, but I'm not sure he believes me."

"Then move in with him and show him how happy he makes you. I really don't get this. The two of you are mates. I'm not saying everything will be easy, and trust me, I know it can be complicated, but why aren't you pushing harder? What do you think will happen if you do?"

"He might shut me out of his life." That was what Thedric feared the most.

Miko leaned forward and grabbed Thedric's hand, squeezing it. "He won't. He's in love with you and wants you as much as you want him. He's just letting his fears talk for him, and that's what you need to deal with. Letting him stew and overthink everything isn't going to help. If anything, it'll make things more complicated."

Miko wasn't wrong. Maybe it was time to stop doing things like this because Les's way wasn't working.

Maybe Thedric's way would.

Thedric got to his feet. Miko grinned and clapped his

hands while Farley whooped. It was an overreaction, but they were happy for Thedric, and he hoped they had good reason to be.

He was getting his mate back, and once he had Les, he was never letting him go.

"He's at home," Farley said, still smiling. "I'm pretty sure the others have left by now, so you should go."

Thedric paused before leaving the office. "Thank you, both of you." He didn't think he'd ever be able to thank them enough for what they'd done.

Miko shrugged. "We're family. It's what family does, isn't it?"

It wasn't what Thedric's family had done until now, but this family was different. Miko, Farley, and everyone else were part of a real family, not like Thedric's parents. "It is," he confirmed before striding out of the office, leaving the two behind.

He had something to do, and he was ready to do it. Hopefully, Les would let him in.

It took way too long for Thedric to reach the shimmering room, but he went straight to Les's house once he was there. The front door was closed, and the house was silent until Thedric knocked. Then Hector barked, and Thedric could hear Les talk to him.

"Niall, if it's you again, I'm going to kick your ass," Les said as he reached the door.

It opened, and they stared at each other. Les didn't seem surprised to see Thedric, which no doubt had to do with his family's intervention. Thedric would have to find a way to thank them if it worked, but first, he had things to say, and he needed Les to listen.

"I hate the mansion," he explained. "I never liked it, and I didn't choose it. It was a wedding gift, and it was easier for Leiana and me to live there because it meant not having to deal with both sets of parents coming after us for not liking their gift. But it was always too big, and it never had any personality. Your house does, and I love it. Here, I feel at home and like I truly belong. More importantly, here I can be myself, which isn't something I've been able to do for the past twenty years. That's what you give me, Les."

Saying the words was hard, but Thedric needed Les to understand. "You feel like you're taking a lot away from me, but it's only the things I don't want, and in exchange, you're giving me the gift of allowing me to be myself. I've never been as happy as I was when I was staying here with you, and I want to move in. I want for us to bond and be together forever, happily ignoring my parents and their world. You freed me. I was never strong enough to do this myself, but now, I can do what I want with my life, and it's thanks to your presence in it. I don't care about the mansion and my parents. I only care about you, me, and what we'll build together."

And he hoped the same went for Les.

Les watched Thedric. He was surprised to realize he believed his mate when he said he didn't care about his parents, his mansion, or anything else he'd leave behind to be with Les. It sounded nuts to him, but what did he know? He'd never been as rich as Thedric, and he never would be. But he'd met Thedric's parents, so he could understand why Thedric was looking forward to leaving them behind. Les wouldn't want a relationship with them if they'd been his parents.

Thedric was an adult. He was older than Les, although since he was a Nix, that was to be expected. He'd lived his life for twenty years, and he knew better than anyone what it would mean for him to stay back or to leave. He'd made his decision.

He wanted to be with Les, and nothing anyone could say

about that would change his mind. It was time for Les to let go of his fear that he was taking more than he was giving. Thedric wouldn't want to be with him if it wasn't what he desired, and Les had to respect that, no matter how little he understood it.

He swallowed. He'd been thinking about this a lot and knew what he wanted. He wanted to make the offer, and he was pretty sure Thedric would say yes, but it felt like it was too soon. Les also wondered if Thedric would ever regret it if they did this.

But he'd just told himself to allow Thedric to make his own decisions, so that was what he'd do.

"I'd like us to bond," he croaked.

Thedric stared. "To bond?"

"Yes. I realize it's a lot to ask, especially considering the situation, but–"

"It's not. It's perfectly natural for you to want to bond. We're mates, after all. It's just that you've been very hesitant, and I can't help but feel like maybe, you don't want this but are asking for it because you think it's what I want."

"It's not. I want us to bond, but I'm scared you might regret it."

"Yet you're asking for it."

"Because I've decided to allow you to make your own decisions. Your parents have kept you under control for decades, and it wasn't fair. I don't want to do the same. You're free to say yes or no, whichever you want, and I won't hold either answer against you." There was no way Les could walk away, even if Thedric said no.

Thedric continued staring for a moment. Les had no idea what to expect, but he was hopeful. Thedric had been all in with their relationship since day one. Les was the one who'd hesitated, but he was done with that.

"My answer is yes," Thedric eventually said.

Les blinked and tried to keep himself in check. "Yes? Wait, are you saying all right to mating? With me?"

Thedric didn't roll his eyes, but Les was pretty sure it was a close thing. "Who else would I want to bond with? You're my mate, Les. If it had been possible, I'd have bonded with you the evening I met you."

"Well, it could have been."

Thedric's smile was gentle. "You needed time, as did I. I don't feel we're rushing into anything, though, and I hope you don't, either. Just like you're not willing to push me into anything, I'm unwilling to let you do things you're not comfortable with."

"I wouldn't have brought it up if I hadn't thought about it and if I wasn't sure of my decision." Les hesitated. He'd researched what bonding with a Nix entailed, even though he'd already known. It would be better to ask Thedric, though. "I know we don't have to drink each other's blood because you're not a shifter."

"You're correct. As long as we both want it, I'll touch your chest and allow the bond to extend and seal. It's hard to explain to someone who can't fully feel it, but it won't hurt, and there will be no blood spilled."

"We both want it." Les certainly did, so he licked his lips and pulled his sweater off. "Let's do it."

Thedric laughed. The sound was enough to tell Les that Thedric wasn't just going along with this to make him happy. He truly wanted to bond.

And they were about to.

Les wanted to give Thedric more reasons to laugh. He wanted to watch him smile, hear him laugh, and make him happy for the rest of his life. If that was all he achieved, then he'd die happy, but he wanted many decades of Thedric before that happened.

"Now?" Thedric asked.

He was already unbuttoning his shirt, so Les doubted he had a problem with it. He was just making sure it was what Les wanted.

"I've thought about it long enough."

"I thought we'd do it in your bedroom."

Les realized what Thedric meant and almost swore. "Right, because bonding is done during sex."

"Not always, but usually, yes, it is. We don't have to do it during sex if you don't want to."

Les surged forward to kiss his mate. "How could I not want sex with you?" He got to his feet and grabbed Thedric's hand. "Let's go."

Thedric laughed again and easily followed. Hector tried to do the same, but Les ordered him to stay on the couch, and for once, he obeyed. Les was relieved because he didn't want to start fighting with his dog right now. He had better things to focus on.

Thedric was beaming when they reached the bedroom. He was at home here since he'd spent many nights in Les's bed and in his arms. This was no different, yet at the same time, it was. It would be the first and only time they bonded.

Les was ready.

He pushed his jeans and underwear down his legs and stepped out of them, stopping to take his socks off on his way to the nightstand. He was eager to make Thedric his, even though he'd been hesitant. He'd never doubted his feelings for Thedric or the way Thedric felt about him. No, he'd doubted the circumstances around them, but he didn't care about any of that anymore.

He peeked at Thedric, glad to see his mate was getting naked, too. He was as eager as Les to do this, which settled something inside Les. Why had he ever doubted Thedric's feelings for him?

Les opened the nightstand drawer and grabbed the bottle

of lube he'd bought after the first time he and Thedric had sex. He'd paid a little more for a more luxurious feeling, and he was glad he had. It felt right to spoil Thedric in the bedroom, too.

When he turned, he stared. Thedric was done getting naked, and like always, he'd taken the time to neatly fold his clothes and hang his shirt on the back of the chair by the door. That wasn't what caught Les's attention, but seeing Thedric completely naked in the middle of the bed they shared was.

It had been Les's bed before, but not anymore. Now, it was theirs.

Thedric's cheeks and upper chest were flushed, and his body was tense as he watched Les. Les watched back for a moment, but he was already hard, and he could see he wasn't the only one.

He climbed onto the bed, moving slowly, both because he was anticipating what was about to happen and because he was scared. It was a massive step forward, and he wanted it no matter how convinced he was of what they were about to do.

Thedric's lips parted as he stared. He looked good enough to eat, and Les didn't know where to start.

He crawled until he hovered over Thedric's dick. Thedric tensed, which Les knew was in anticipation. He could read his mate by now, which made it easier to know what Thedric liked and disliked.

He continued to move slowly as he opened the lube. Thedric enjoyed things that way until they got to the crucial moments of lovemaking. Then, he always demanded that Les go faster and fuck him harder, which Les was more than happy to go along with.

Today wouldn't be any different.

Thedric opened his legs to welcome Les. Les leaned closer, slipping his hand between Thedric's legs as he wrapped his lips around Thedric's cock. Thedric gave a tiny thrust upward, then stilled as if he didn't want to overwhelm Les. They'd done this several times already, but they were both out of practice when it came to sex and happy to relearn everything with each other.

Thedric reached out to touch Les's cheek. Les tried to smile, but with Thedric's cock in his mouth, he couldn't, so instead, he ran his tongue along the underside of Thedric's cock. At the same time, he massaged Thedric's hole, determined to drive him to beg before this was over.

He did everything he could to make that happen, thinking back to when he was young and did this on a more regular basis. He'd learned some tricks back then and didn't hesitate to use them all.

He sucked on the head of Thedric's cock while he opened him up with his fingers. Thedric stayed still in the beginning, but soon, he writhed under Les. He hadn't begged yet, but he'd buried his fingers into Les's hair and kept pulling, then pushing as if he wasn't sure whether he wanted Les to continue what he was doing or for him to move up and kiss him.

Seeing him like that made Les want to rush, but he forced himself to take his time, even though his cock was so hard he could probably use it to pound nails. He ignored it and focused on Thedric, swallowing his cock as deeply as he could without making himself gag.

Thedric's back came off the bed, and he pulled hard on Les's hair. "Please, stop."

There was the begging Les had wanted.

He let go of Thedric's cock, but he kept his fingers in place, moving them in and out as he watched Thedric pant. "What?"

"It's too much. If you want to bond during sex, you need to stop using your mouth."

Les pushed his fingers as deep as they could go. "But not my fingers?"

Thedric moaned. "I'd rather have your cock in me, but I can do it like this, too."

Les wasn't on board for that, at least not on this occasion. Maybe he'd see if he could make Thedric come just with his mouth and fingers next time, though. "Ready?"

Thedric's gaze was tender. "I've been ready for this since the first time I saw you." He wasn't talking about sex.

Les's heart raced. He slid his fingers out of Thedric, hoping his mate was ready. The last thing he wanted was to hurt Thedric, but on this, too, he'd need to trust Thedric. He knew whether or not he was ready to take Les in.

Thedric's eyes were incredibly wide, and Les slithered up his body. He pressed kisses along Thedric's thighs, in the place where they met his groin, skirted around his cock so as not to torture him, then kissed up the blond trail of hair on his lower stomach and to his belly button. Next came his chest and nipples, and when their lips finally met, Les was in position with Thedric's thighs held open on top of his.

He wrapped his fingers around his cock and held it up, aimed at Thedric's ass. He let go once the head of his cock pressed against the opening and gently pushed. Thedric relaxed, and Les slid inside smoothly, not stopping until he and Thedric were pressed together.

He paused and looked at his mate. This was it. In seconds, they'd be bonded together, one as far as most people were concerned.

"Okay?" he asked, needing to know. Thedric had to feel as overwhelmed as he was, right?

Thedric nodded and put his hands on Les's shoulders. "Never been better."

Les started to move again. Thedric clung to him, and it felt as if he'd never let go. Les knew enough about what came next, and while his rhythm faltered when he grabbed Thedric's right hand from his shoulder and lifted it to his chest, he never stopped moving.

"Thedric," he breathed out, and Thedric understood.

Thedric's hand was like a brand on Les's skin. It started glowing, and when it turned warmer and warmer, Les hoped it wouldn't be too long because he didn't think he could last. He took Thedric's cock in his hand, grinned when Thedric groaned, then whimpered as the touch on his chest turned painful.

It only lasted a few seconds. The glow became so strong Les had to close his eyes, then feelings that weren't his slammed into him. It was overwhelming. The pleasure, the satisfaction, the love—all of it mirrored what Les felt but was also so different he knew it didn't come from him.

Les bit his lower lip so he wouldn't scream, then remembered they were alone in the house and allowed himself to make noise. The hand on his chest stopped glowing and the warmth disappeared, but Les barely noticed because he was coming inside his mate, his pleasure mingling with Thedric's until he didn't know where he ended and Thedric started.

He didn't care.

Les was careful as he lowered his body on top of Thedric's. Thedric wrapped his arms around him instantly, almost as if he didn't want to let go. Les felt a bit tender, and not just physically. His emotions were all over the place, and it felt good to pause for a moment and enjoy what had happened. There was so *much* to feel and make sense of.

He mentally prodded at the new sensation in his mind. It could only be Thedric, and he knew he was right when Thedric chuckled.

Hello, my love, whispered through Les's mind.

He grinned like an idiot. He wasn't sure how that worked, but it wouldn't stop him from trying. *Hello.*

Thedric laughed. "We're bonded."

And for once, Les wasn't terrified of what it would mean.

CHAPTER SEVEN

Thedric didn't do birthday parties. He did birthday dinners, where everyone went to eat out at an expensive restaurant, politely said happy birthday, and went home. Yet he'd already gone to two home birthday parties over a few weeks.

He looked around. Not only had his family become bigger than it ever had been, but apparently, it now included an entire pride. He wasn't quite sure how he was supposed to be related to them, but he'd been dragged to the birthday party of a man called Jordan. If Thedric remembered correctly, Jordan was mated to Nestor, who was Jude's brother. Jude was Flynn's mate, and since Thedric was mated to Flynn's uncle, it meant he absolutely had to be there.

Thinking about it made his head spin.

He was getting used to having many more people in his life, but a birthday party with an entire pride of people he'd never met before was still a lot, which was why he was hanging around in a corner, holding a drink and nodding at people when they walked past. Les was here, of course, but he'd seen someone he needed to talk to and had left Thedric on his own for a bit.

That was all right. Thedric wasn't terrified the way he might have been before. He knew that if he became too uncomfortable, he could leave, and Les wouldn't be offended. He doubted Jordan, the birthday boy, would be either since, apart from saying hello when Thedric had first arrived, they'd never talked to each other.

But it felt good to be here. This might not be the kind of parties Thedric was used to, but it was his life now, and he loved it. He wanted to show Les that he didn't miss the posh parties he used to go to with his parents. If anything, he was much more comfortable here, even surrounded by a bunch of people he didn't know. These people were real, unlike Thedric's parents and the rest of their social circle.

"Everything okay?" Miko asked, suddenly appearing next to Thedric.

Thedric smiled at his nephew. The two of them were closer than ever. It was as if Thedric had never been out of Miko's life, although he suspected their relationship would have been different if he'd been there since the beginning. They might not have been close friends the way they were now. Thedric was happy with his life as it was, and he never wanted it to change.

"It's a lot," he confessed.

Miko nodded. "I get it. I mean, our family is pretty small, and while I've always had Farley, I didn't always have this many friends. I guess they came along after we met Nestor."

That was a surprise. "You're always so open to people. I thought you'd have many friends."

"I do. Well, most of them could be called acquaintances. They're the people I went to school with, things like that. But the ones I'm closest to are Farley and Nestor, and Farley and I didn't use to have much to do with the pride until Nestor met his mate."

"Who's a pride member, right?" Thedric thought he remembered that correctly.

"Yeah, Jordan. He's a tiger shifter, and even though he and Nestor don't live with the pride, they're both pride members."

It was like a massive family, and apparently, they'd all adopted Thedric. Thedric wasn't sure he understood why, but he wasn't about to protest.

For the first time, he felt like he belonged.

He wouldn't let anyone take this away from him. Luckily, he doubted anyone would try. His parents had attempted to contact both him and Leiana and had pulled her parents into the mix. They were all angry about the divorce, so much so that Thedric's father had contacted the divorce lawyers to threaten them. Thankfully, they didn't care who Thedric's father was and how much money he had, and the divorce was well on its way to being final, which was a relief for everyone involved. Leiana was talking about selling the house, which would be perfectly fine with Thedric. He hadn't gone back except to pack his bags and move the things he couldn't bear to leave behind. She still lived there, but it wouldn't be for long.

Leiana would always have a place in Thedric's life, and he was grateful that Les understood that. They were friends, and that would never change. Thedric would always feel responsible for her, and he'd make sure she was all right, but they could finally live their lives as they wanted. The twenty years they'd shared hadn't been unhappy, but it was time for both of them to be happy.

Which, for Thedric, apparently included attending birthday parties.

He looked around the room and noticed that Les was still talking to the person who'd waved him closer before. Les had mentioned it was the alpha, so Thedric wasn't about to bother him, but when Les looked up and noticed him watching, he waved and gave him a little smile. Les mirrored the gesture, and Thedric's heart felt like it was about to explode.

This was his life now. No matter how overwhelming it was, he wouldn't want it any other way. He had everything he'd never allowed himself to hope for and everything he'd never dreamed he could have. No matter how Les felt about taking him away from his life, Thedric had never been so happy.

Since he was here, he decided it might be time to get to know some more of the people who were now part of his life. His drink was gone, and he could talk to people as he got another one and maybe a slice of cake. His mother wouldn't be there to tell him he'd get fat if he ate cake.

Hell, maybe he'd get two slices.

"I'm going to get another drink," he told his nephew. "Do you need anything?"

"I don't think so, but if you see Farley, will you tell him I'm looking for him? I can't find him."

Thedric nodded and stepped away from the wall. The room was full of people, so it took a bit of maneuvering to get to the tables where drinks and food were available. He only got one slice of cake, then a drink, and he found himself unsure about how to eat the cake with both hands busy.

He noticed a small table in the corner that seemed empty and made his way there, putting down everything before he noticed that Farley was hiding behind the table.

"Farley?" he asked, alarmed by the expression on Farley's face.

It was shock. Whatever had happened, Farley was in shock, which meant Thedric needed to take care of him. That was perfectly fine with him, but he wasn't quite sure what to do.

Farley looked at him. "I saw him."

Thedric had no idea who Farley was talking about. "Saw who? Miko? He was looking for you." But that didn't sound right. Why would seeing Miko shock Farley to the point where he was hiding behind a table?

Farley shook his head. "Not him. My mate. I saw my mate."

Well, that would certainly explain the shock.

About the Author

Catherine is the creator of several series, most of them paranormal, including the Whitedell Pride Series and the Gillham Pack Series. While she graduated in translation, she decided to go the writer's way because it was more fun to create her own stories and characters.

She's been living in Italy for more than twenty years, but she's a daughter of the North—Belgium to be precise—and she misses it so much that she's already planning to move back.

She loves pizza—probably too much—her son, her pets, and of course, books. She sneaks some reading time into her schedule every time she has five minutes free from writing, demands from her various pets and son, and lastly, housework.

Connect with her:

lievens.catherine@gmail.com
BookBub: https://www.bookbub.com/authors/catherine-lievens
Website: https://authorcatherinelievens.com/
Facebook: https://www.facebook.com/catherine.lievens.9
Facebook Group: https://www.facebook.com/groups/411788002341528/
Twitter: https://twitter.com/authorCLievens
Newsletter: http://eepurl.com/c-uvKn

www.ingramcontent.com/pod-product-compliance
Lightning Source LLC
LaVergne TN
LVHW020643100826
845148LV00012B/2318

* 9 7 8 1 4 8 7 4 3 8 6 2 3 *